STEADFAST

DANIELLE NORMAN

I'd like to dedicate this to Stuart Reardon, although you have no clue that I exist. I would like to believe that if I were younger and thinner and not happily married or you were in to older chunky chicks and not in love with your girl then maybe just maybe our worlds would have collided.

STEADFAST

Danielle Norman

— SOMETIMES YOU WIN;
SOMETIMES YOU LEARN.
UNKNOWN

Chapter One

HOLLAND

To say that I was pissed was an understatement. The last thing I wanted to do was to sit in some boring ass town hall meeting. I blamed this on my sisters. They strong-armed me to coming by saying things like, "We always do it," "It's your turn," and "You're one-third owner." Okay, all of that was true, but it didn't change the fact that this was the last place I wanted to be.

I walked up the steps to the old Geneva community center, which I hadn't been inside since I was little. The last time I'd been here was in first grade and my dad forced me to join Girl Scouts. Thank god, Dad only made me do that for one year, but remembering the way he used to pretend to eat whatever concoction I had made or how he'd worn that tacky scarf I had knitted with popsicle sticks made my heart heavy with loss. People would have thought my badges were the equivalent to the Nobel Peace Prize, he revered them so much.

Staring up at the night sky, I blew him a kiss before pulling the door open. The difference between the cold fresh night air and the heated stale air of the old building was heavy. I sneezed as the smell of dust burning on a radiator that didn't get used often tickled my nose.

Moving into the room, I smiled at the sight of so many people, for a moment, I felt like I was in an episode of Peanuts. You know how they always show Snoopy talking and it sounds like, *wah, wah, wah, wah.* That was what it sounded like to me. So many people were talking that nothing seemed coherent.

I removed my coat and hung it on a peg in the back of the room before making my way to a couple of ranchers who had been close friends with my dad. I didn't get to say anything before a whoosh of cold air blew in, causing everyone to turn and my ire to grow. Great, just fucking great, if it wasn't Dick Brooks. Yes, I knew his name wasn't really Dick, but it was so much more fun to call him that instead of Reid. In my typical greeting, I moved to lift my middle finger, but he was faster, and he grabbed my hand, holding it down.

"Don't. You know what that means, don't you?" His deep voice sent warm shivers down my neck.

"Yeah, it means fuck you," I hissed.

"Exactly, and if you aren't careful, I might think you are propositioning me."

"You wish."

Reid took several steps back and looked up and then down my body, taking me in. "Maybe, maybe not." He strode off, leaving me with my mouth gaping wide open. Fuck. I was seldom at a loss for words, but for some reason, I had been finding myself at a loss a lot more often when he was around.

"All right, everyone, if you could please take your seats," a man in a fancy business suit said. Suit, really? Geneva was not a suit kind of town, unless it was for your funeral. Even for church, we wore jeans. I already distrusted this man, whomever he was.

I followed the crowd to the rows of folding chairs that

had been set up, and tried to sit as far from Reid as I could but ended up about three seats in front of him. I turned and glared at him. If looks could kill, I would be decapitating that motherfucker right here in this tiny building. He locked eyes with me and was stunned. *Dick*, I mouthed.

"We're glad to see so many of you here tonight. First, I'd like to make some introductions. I'm councilman Shane Stuart, to my left is Johnson Holbrook, and to my right is his son Michael Holbrook."

"As in Johnson Holbrook, the land developer?" Mr. Kirby asked. He was one of the men I'd been headed toward when Reid had come in and he owned a small ranch up the road from mine.

"Yes, he is." The councilman waited for a second, as if expecting us to applaud, but no one was clapping.

I stood. "So, I'm assuming that Michael works for Johnson? In what capacity?"

"Good question," someone behind me whispered, and for some strange reason I had a feeling that it had been Reid.

"I handle all contracts for the company," Michael said.

"And you, councilman?"

"I'm not involved with their business at all. I'm just the representative for this area."

I sat and felt a hand squeeze my shoulder, glancing over, I saw the gnarled, callused fingers of one of the older ranchers.

"We're here because of an expansion road that is being built to connect I-95 and State Road 417. This new road would exit southbound on ninety-five approximately four miles before the current State Road 46 exit."

I tried to envision these locations. I didn't take I-95 very often but . . .

"Excuse me, if I'm hearing you right, it seems as if that trajectory would take the new proposed road right over our community." I looked back to find Reid standing there, arms folded across his broad chest, and his eyes sparkling with an angry glint.

"If everyone will hold their questions until the end, we might answer them as we go along and save us all time," Stuart said, somewhat snarky. "At a recent cabinet meeting, the Secretary of the Transportation Commission went over the proposed plans, the companies that had bid on the project, and the lowest bidder was Johnson Holbrook."

I was uncomfortable and totally wishing that my sisters were here. The hairs on the back of my neck were standing on end, you know like when they say, someone is walking across your grave.

"Please." The councilman held up one hand. "See the possibilities and how this will benefit the intra-community. Right now it takes you, what? At least thirty minutes to get to a hospital? How many of you have to take a cooler to the grocery store just for products like ice cream and popsicles because you can't get them home before they melt? This road will help you get places faster so the direct benefit to the community is a bonus." Several of us grumbled because, like me, they were probably okay going without ice cream and all knew that the paramedics were only seven minutes away. "But for inter-community, the road enhancement will benefit the University of Central Florida, helping ease traffic to its more than fifty-thousand students. It will offer alternative options for moving traffic from I-95 when there are shutdowns or easing the flow from the Atlantic side inland." The councilman paused for several seconds, and something in me told me the man had been in theater when he was in school. He definitely knew how to wield a dramatic silence. "As you can all see, this has been thoroughly thought out and the benefits are overwhelming. We have contracts for many of you that are an above fair price."

"Above fair for what?" I asked, but I didn't stand to ask it.

"Please," Councilman Stuart commanded, "wait until the end. We have a copy of the proposal for everyone who's affected. Some properties may only be asked to sell a small parcel of land so that we can sink a support beam, others may be larger parcels to feed a new exit ramp into the town of Geneva. With all of this said, I would like to turn the floor over to Mr. Holbrook."

"Thank you, Shane. As your councilman clearly stated this is a done deal, ladies and gentlemen, now it is up to you how much you profit from this deal. Once we begin, the state will declare eminent domain, for those of you unfamiliar with the term, it means that for the greater good of the community and people. It is believed that this expansion road will decrease traffic on State Road 46, which has a high casualty rate due to the long straight distance of a single lane. The expansion will also enhance the appeal for future development to improve property values and economics."

"In other words, it will destroy our small town," I chided.

"What is your name?" Johnson Holbrook asked, directing his gaze straight at me.

I pushed out a heavy breath and stood. "Holland Kelly, and I want to know exactly how you've been developing this idea. I would think that it would take more than a single cabinet meeting for a road that connects from an interstate, which is state owned, to connect to a state road, which is also state owned to be approved, right? You're talking about appropriating funds from the Florida Transportation Commission—"

"Young lady," Oh, I hated when people used that condescending term, "I'm glad to hear that you know how to use Google, but perhaps you should learn how things really work."

"Well, why don't you enlighten us, I'm sure your fancy

education that affords your fancy suits can teach us poor country folks a thing or two."

When Shane Stuart reached into his briefcase and pulled out a gavel, I almost laughed. He had a real, honest to goodness, fucking gavel. "Enough, Miss Kelly, you may sit." He banged it three times.

"No, Shane, let the chit finish." Holbrook held out one hand as if placating him.

"I'll be the first to agree that Holland is fiery but do not disrespect her." Reid almost shouted from behind me. "You are attempting to take away her home and livelihood, so I would think that you would be a bit more professional." I smiled, a bit shocked by Reid's defense of me.

"And you are?" Shane asked.

"Reid Brooks, I own Old Kentucky Stables."

"Mr. Brooks," Johnson Holbrook interrupted. "It's very nice to meet you."

Reid just nodded and then sat. So, I followed suit.

"Now, let's continue. The reason we asked you all to come here this evening was to discuss this proposal and how we hope we'll be able to come to some sort of agreement. With eminent domain, the state appointed third party—in this case, that would be me—is only required to pay the just value. If you are not sure what the just value of your property is, look at your tax records. As we all know that never shows our true property value. At least for me"—Holbrook let out a fake chuckle—"it says that my home is only worth one-fifth the going rate. I'm sure that the property taxes are the same for all of you especially since you have such large parcels of land." I glanced around and saw several ranchers nodding, including Mr. Kirby and Mr. Brown. Damn it, he had their attention. "What I want to do now is to make you an offer that is far above what the state would pay you because, let's face it, the faster we get this settled, the less amount of money it costs me having to pay the interest fees on the loan advance until the state reimburses me." He let out his stupid damn chuckle again. "We all want to get through this inevitable mess with the least amount of stress, and I'm sure that each of you wants to be compensated for your property." Several people in the crowd agreed, but some let out grumbles of disapproval, which did not go unnoticed by Holbrook. "Folks, you don't have to accept my offer, but if you don't, I would suggest hiring attorneys and try your luck in fighting eminent domain."

"I understand that we can't fight eminent domain, but how do we know that eminent domain is inevitable?" I asked.

"Young lady, I'm tired of your outbursts. The councilman is here with me as your public official to represent you and announce eminent domain," Holbrook snapped at me.

"Funny, you're the one that is telling us about it," I snapped back.

"Miss Kelly, one more outburst and you'll be asked to leave so that the other residents may have a clear understanding of what is going on," Shane Stuart threatened.

More like I'll be told to leave so they don't have anyone asking the right questions.

I sat.

"Michael, if you will please hand out the packets," Holbrook directed his son. "He will call your name, if he does, then your property is being affected by the expansion."

"Technically, everyone is being affected because everyone is part of this town." I turned in my chair because, as much as I hated to admit it, I liked that Reid considered himself as part of the community. "The effects on the animals will be catastrophic not just in attitudes for handling but in their lifestyle and breeding. Crops will be affected by the emissions in the air. Would you want your vegetables or fruits grown along a highway? Think of the pollution that would be absorbed into them or into the soil and water? This is more than just the few hundred acres, this is an entire town."

"Well, son—" Holbrook began.

"I'm not your son. I already told you that my name is Reid Brooks."

"Reid," Michael called out and walked over and handed Reid a packet. "And, Holland Kelly, here's yours." Michael tossed it to me. He continued working his way around the room.

Holbrook began again, "Well, Reid, I'm not at liberty to offer the others compensation, I'm sorry. Now, let's go on. Inside your packets is a contract with our offered price. We've also included a pen so that you could sign the agreement stating that you accept that elevated price. It doesn't mean your property is sold today. Call it a good-faith offer on our part. You see, what it does, is guarantee that you will not be offered less than that amount for your property."

I opened my packets and let out a gasp, the asshole wanted almost one-fourth of our ranch. "I thought you said small parcels?"

"I said some areas would only require small parcels. Unfortunately, the area over your ranch isn't one of them." I swore to god there was a smirk on Holbrook's face.

"You asshole. You want me to give up a quarter of my property? That is unacceptable, and I refuse to even consider it!"

"I'm sorry, but you don't have a choice."

"Bullshit, I'll fight you, you pig."

"Miss Kelly, you might want to be careful, you're treading into awfully dangerous territory. Please understand that I don't have to offer you that elevated amount and I can rescind it at any time."

"Is that a threat? Are you really threatening me in front of half the town?" The balls on this guy were huge.

"Calm down, Holland, this isn't the place to fight him," Reid whispered from behind me. I turned and shot daggers at him. Finally not able to think of any words, I flipped him off.

"Enough, Miss Kelly." Councilman Stuart banged his gavel. "Everyone has their packets, and I urge you to read them and sign them before you leave. We will stay for a few moments to collect the forms and answer any questions you may have that didn't get answered because Miss Kelly couldn't refrain from interrupting. Miss Kelly, you are excused." He banged his gavel once more, then stood, and slipped it back into his briefcase.

I needed to get to Reid because I wanted to see his packet, but before I could make my way out of my row, Holbrook stopped me. "Keep it up, Miss Kelly, and I'm sure we can have the road moved to go over the entire Kelly Ranch."

"It will never happen."

"Never say never. The people in this town look up to Mr. Brooks, so I only have to convince him to sell his measly five acres." With that, he smiled and turned to Stuart, effectively dismissing me.

I bit my tongue so hard it almost bled, reined in the urge to throttle the man, and turned to find Reid. He was standing by the door and several ranchers were already gathered around him as if he were the Mayor of Munchkin Land. I came to a stop just outside the circle and fought to gain some control and listened.

"Don't do anything yet, let me call my attorney and do some research. I think it's pretty clear that none of us are willing to sign anything, so that makes us stronger together than we are divided. Please hear me out before anyone agrees to anything. If he comes to you or tries to get you to sign this form again just tell him that you'll need to have an attorney go over it."

"Can't afford no attorney," Mr. Brown said.

"Me neither," another rancher agreed.

"I'm not asking you to. My attorney will handle it for all of us."

Johnson Holbrook had finally noticed our little gathering and was trying to extricate himself from the councilman. Oh, crap, I didn't want him to overhear anything, especially since Reid was still talking. "Trust me, I have—"

"Hey, Reid," I said a bit too loudly. "Hi, Mr. Cameron, Mr. Brown, Mr. Kirby." Darting my eyes to my left repeatedly, I tried to get Reid to turn and look. "It was so nice seeing you all this evening."

"Holland, can you give us a few minutes?" Mr. Kirby asked.

But Reid had finally caught on to what I was trying to do. "Holland, I wanted to talk with you. Gentlemen"—he turned toward Johnson—"Mr. Holbrook, if you all will excuse us." Reid walked over and held out one hand to me, palm up. "Shall we?"

I stared down at it as if it were a trap. "Shall we what?"

"Go over there and talk." He motioned toward a corner. I nodded, and he led the way. Once we were out of earshot of everyone else, he said, "Thank you. Nice save. I don't want Holbrook getting a heads-up before we can get all of our shit together."

"What shit?"

"I don't know yet, but that's where you come in. I'd like your help to figure out what we can do to stop this because something isn't sitting right with me."

"He just threatened to take all of my land if I don't fall in line. Reid, he wants to take a quarter of our property for this. The quarter that houses the barn."

His eyes widened a bit and he pulled the packet from my

hands. "He can't seriously think you would give up the stables, paddock, and training area."

"He does, and he threatened to take it all if I didn't agree. It's one thing for me to lose my tiny apartment above the stables, but I can't let him take my sisters' houses."

"But you'll give up yours?"

"If I have to."

"Well, I'm not selling without a fight, and I don't think you'll have to sell either. Will you meet me tomorrow so we can go over this paperwork and come up with a plan? If you don't feel better about all of this when we're done, I'll do whatever I can to help you."

I thought about his offer and let a bit of hope in. Maybe I would be able to keep my stables. "Fine. What time?"

"Anytime, I'll be home all day."

I wasn't sure this was a great idea . . . me on enemy territory. But right then Reid didn't feel like an enemy, he felt like my only ally. "Okay. I have a few lessons tomorrow, so it will be later in the afternoon, is that all right?"

"Fine by me. We can have dinner together." I stared at him and didn't say a word. What? He and I having dinner together was not only a no, it was a hell no. It would feel too personal. "Holland, I said that we—"

"Stop, I ignored what you said just fine the first time. It'll be before six, I have dinner with my family then."

"What a coincidence, so do I. I'll have enough for both of us just in case you're running late. See you then." Reid didn't wait for me to answer or tell him it would be a cold day in Hell before I had dinner with him. Nope, he just strode through the doors, once again leaving me at a loss for words.

Chapter Two

HOLLAND

I wasn't a morning person. Okay, mornings had nothing to do with it. I wasn't a people person. Fine, that wasn't true either. The fact was, I wasn't a Reid Brooks person. I had just stayed up most of the night tossing and turning and debating whether or not talking to Reid was a good idea. That made me extra cranky.

I peered out the small dormer window from my studio apartment above the Iron Horse Stables, the stables my family owned, and saw him standing in the sunroom or whatever that room was called holding a cup of coffee. The man looked like he was way too happy to greet the day.

I gave him the middle finger, and then I gave him another one for being such an asshat. Okay, he couldn't see me, but it wasn't about him seeing me, it was more about making me feel better, which it did.

Ever since he moved next door, something about my world seemed off. The truth was, he didn't belong here. He belonged back where he came from . . . Kentucky, home of the Kentucky Derby, racehorses, men who wore ascots, and women who wore frilly dresses. He had no business here in Podunk, Florida.

Our one stoplight town was full of people who reused their butter bowls and jelly jars. It wasn't because they didn't have the money for new ones; it was because they understood the values in things. Most days, you could drive through the back roads and see sheets hanging on clotheslines because nothing beat air-drying. We wore cowboy boots and Wranglers, lived for John Deere and Tractor Supply, and preferred Western riding and barrel racing. In other words, Reid Brooks did not belong here.

Letting out another yawn, I finished getting ready and then pulled on my boots. After grabbing my peacoat, I headed down the stairs. The stables were temperature controlled, but they were still cold in the mornings—not like Canada cold, but cold for Central Florida. We had been dropping down into the thirties at night, which was glacial for us.

After turning on the lights, I filled several buckets of oats, added some sliced apples and carrots, and then started feeding the horses. I began with Balthazar. He had been my dad's stallion and was the oldest in our stable, so patience wasn't his strong point. Once he was taken care of, I moved on to Madam Mim, Ursula, Jafar, and the others. Yes, we had a penchant for naming our horses after Disney villains. But I always saved Sher Khan for last, he was mine, opening his stall door, he whinnied several times before leaning toward me so I could rub his gray muzzle. The horse was a beast at sixteen hands, but what he didn't let most people know was that he was a gentle giant.

"Morning, fellow." He shoved his head toward my coat pocket, looking for his apple. He wasn't dumb; he knew that I was a sucker for his charm. "Here you go." I held my jacket pocket out wide so he could grab it before moving to his feed pail and pouring in the oats.

While the horses ate, I got started on my morning chores of mucking out the stalls and filling them with fresh hay. When that was done, I saddled Khan and the two of us broke free, which was our morning ritual. I let him run at his own pace because I knew how much I enjoyed that feeling of freedom first thing in the morning as well. It was almost as if my soul needed to be free after being locked up all night.

When Khan and I were in the open there were no cares in the world and no asshole neighbor. Shit, why did I have to think about him?

"Come on, Khan, let's go." Digging my heels into his sides, Khan took off at breakneck speed, cutting across the pasture before looping back up around the two houses. The one off to the left belonged to my older sister, London, and I trotted past it and up to the main house. It was where I grew up, my childhood home, and my sister, Paris, lived there with Asher, her husband. I finally slowed Sher Khan as the stables came back into view, and he kicked up some dirt with his refusal before giving in. I dismounted and walked him the rest of the way to the barn as part of his cool-down process. I didn't lead him to his stall, instead, I guided him to the drain bay so I could brush him down.

If Khan had been a racehorse, his name would have been Street Walker because the animal was a whore—well, a whore for attention. "Okay, dude, stop shoving your body against me. I'm rubbing you down." He slid his giant head under my hands again to remind me not to stop petting. "You aren't a cat, you freak." I placed a quick peck on his muzzle. "Go, you're done."

I led him back to his stall and then headed up to talk with my sisters. All my life each of us had had our place on the ranch. Mine was in the stables, curled up on a bale of hay talking to the horses. I didn't care about friends, not human friends, why should I, when I had the truest of friends right here in each stall.

When Daddy couldn't get me interested in the ranch, and I never went boy crazy, I think that was when he realized that my love truly was horses. So he built the stables and training area then signed me up for Western riding classes.

Opening the door to the house, I was greeted by the giggles of Tera, my niece. "Morning, sunshine, don't you look like a mess?"

"She's just finished her breakfast." London moved to wipe Tera's face, but Tera was having none of it.

"That's it, girl, give her hell."

"Hey, watch it, she's starting to repeat shit," London admonished me.

I raised one eyebrow. "Did you even listen to yourself?"

"No, why?"

"Never mind." I laughed. "So, last night's meeting was a clusterfuck." I plopped down into a seat and took the cup of coffee Paris handed me.

"Why? What happened? It's too early for the gossip mill to be in full swing yet." London and Paris both took seats opposite me.

I curled one leg under myself and tugged on the sleeves of my sweatshirt to cover my cold hands before cupping the mug in front of me. Once I was settled, I started at the beginning and ended with how worried I was they were going to have to gather bail money for me because I was ready to bury those men's bodies.

"Wait, you lost your temper? How shocking." London smirked.

"Please. I admit my faults even though they are few." London threw her hands over her head as if to protect herself. "What are you doing?"

"Shielding myself from lightning, you know God is going to strike you down for that one."

"Ha, ha."

"So, what's the plan now?"

"This is where I seriously contemplated the demise of both of you, I have to meet with Dick Brooks today so that he and I can formulate a plan." Paris let out a giggle, and I shot her the stink-eye. Then London joined in laughing. I pushed my chair back and moved to get up.

"Stay. Tell us about the plan." London reached out for me.

"Not totally sure yet. We're going to meet and see what we can come up with. Sort of a divide-and-conquer thing, I think, but don't hold your breath that it will actually do any good."

"Why not?" London asked.

"He isn't from here, so when it comes down to it, how hard will he really fight to save our town? I can't see him going to the mats for us."

"I don't know about that. I think that he has found peace here, and I think the two of you are more alike than you care to acknowledge," Paris said as she gave me a wink. "If you found a place you loved, I don't think it would matter whether you grew up there or had lived there one year, it would be your sanctuary, and you would fight."

"Awww, to be a fly on the wall when you two put your heads together."

"Screw you both, this isn't funny." I flipped them off and then strode out.

Heading to my small one bedroom apartment, I made a mental list of things to do, and most of them required good old Google. As soon as I walked in, I snagged my laptop and then set it on my kitchen island. I turned the television on for background noise and then started my internet search.

Eminent domain was the first thing I pulled up, and as I

read, I rolled a pen between my fingers as if it were a tiny baton, only stopping the motion long enough to make random notes. According to the website, most of the time land must be taken by state or federal authorities, but occasionally, a third party can be delegated. In those cases, there are contracts showing that the third party will devote the property to public or civic use and in some cases economic development.

I bounced the tip of the pen against the counter as I flipped through site after site and my hopes elevated. When I began reading about bad coverage of eminent domain and how many states had started refraining from using it because the last two cases that went to the supreme court had caused such a public outcry that many states had even rewritten their laws concerning eminent domain.

I made a note about the supreme court rulings over the city of New London, Connecticut, and Norwood, Ohio, and then I made another note of the 2006 executive order signed by President Bush . . .

Chapter Three

REID

I wasn't sure if it was even possible for me to start my morning without Holland Kelly's spitfire attitude. The little demon spawn did something to set my world right. Maybe I was a glutton for punishment, but every morning, I sat in my sunroom, holding a pad and my charcoal as I waited for her to give me the bird. She did it every morning, and every morning, I drank my coffee and sketched while I waited for it.

I constantly glanced between the pad and the window, not wanting to miss that moment she showed her attitude. It always made me laugh. The time she mooned me and I was frozen between yelling at her and asking her to do it again. I ended up not doing either because if she knew I could see her, she'd never do it again.

This morning I had waited for her shadow, and once it flashed in front of her window, I paused and just like clockwork, she appeared. Today, I hadn't just gotten one middle finger—I had gotten two. It was probably a precursor for later, she was already in rare form.

I had returned to my sketch, until the old clock that hung on the wall moved, and the little bird came out and gave a cuckoo alerting that it was six a.m. and time for me to start my day. I had wanted to see Holland ride by on her gray gelding since I had a sketch that I wanted to finish and the angles seemed to be off in my mind. But I also had a shitload of things to get done if I wanted to be ready for her when she got here later today. If I knew her, she would spend her free time on her computer, trying to discover as much as she could about eminent domain. The one thing that woman was . . . was intelligent, and she would relish in knowing more than I did about the topic. I wasn't having it.

"Morning, Syd." He always beat me here, but that was because he lived in the apartment above the stables and never actually slept.

"Good morning, I got Nostradamus saddled up for you."

"Thanks." I zipped my jacket and pulled on some gloves as I headed into Nostradamus's stall, my one non-Thorough-bred. The moment I saw the Andalusian, we had bonded. There was something about him—maybe it was his warrior physique, he was seventeen hands, after all—but whatever it was, he was mine. Like the prophet he's named after, the horse knew I was his.

He let me walk him out of his stall and then climb into the saddle. Once I was settled, we were out. Each morning, the two of us enjoyed our ride. Sometimes I saw Holland, and sometimes I gave her a hard time, but it wasn't something I actively sought to do.

Nostradamus didn't have to be directed, he knew our route and that we covered my property in a clockwise fash-ion. Since I didn't have small animals, I kept the beauty of the property with a split rail fence. In a trot, Nostradamus led me around, occasionally stopping when I needed to dismount and check a fence post or a beam. Occasionally, a deer or some other animal got caught and thrashed their way through, knocking a beam or two loose, so I kept a special saddlebag full of supplies with me just in case I needed to mend something.

As Nostradamus and I approached the end of our ride, which took me along the property line between my and the Kellys' properties, something about the thought of not starting my day seeing Holland's whiskey-colored eyes had me wanting to do another lap but there were chores to get done.

I stepped down, and before heading inside, I ran my fingers through Nostradamus's black mane, thanking him for the ride, and then I handed him off to Syd.

"How was your ride?" Syd asked.

"It was good. I don't miss the Kentucky snow, but I do miss cool mornings and breathing in the crisp morning air. There's nothing like it on the back of a horse. I wish we had more of them here."

"Bite your tongue. Winter happens about the third week of January, and that is long enough in my book."

"If it were longer, it would kill off some bugs. Couldn't you handle a few less fleas?" Syd didn't answer. "Ticks?" He still didn't say anything. "Mosquitos?"

"I could do with fewer of those blood suckers. They ruin my summer evenings. As soon as I light up my cigar, they are all over me like white on rice." I scratched my head, trying to comprehend his statement, white on rice? Whatever.

I was still thinking about it when he asked, "So, what do you want me to focus on today?"

"Got a call from the Winterheimers last night, they've decided to put their horses, Wellfleet and Nantucket, into claims races this year, so they want us to increase their exercise and work on carving some seconds off their long stretch."

"Got it. I'll have Noah get started on that right away." Noah was a rider who I had come in. He was small and had the build of a jockey, so it helped us to get a better reading when we were working on time trials. "Anything else? Did you ever hear from Slipper's owner?"

"Nope. I sent him a certified letter with the total amount of veterinary costs plus boarding and rehabilitation but he hasn't answered. He has until the first or he forfeits ownership. I reckon we won't hear from him. The guy's a dick and is only worried about money, so what does he want with a horse that fractured a cannon bone? It's a pet now, and he has no time for pets." I walked over to the chestnut Thoroughbred. When she had heard my voice, she came to her stall door and waited. "Morning, beautiful, how's that leg feeling, the cold weather making it hurt?" I opened the latch to her stall and moved inside so I could rub my hands along the bandages. "It doesn't feel like it's flared up, which is good. When you get a chance, let's get an X-ray on her leg."

"Will do." Syd wrote a few notes in the small pad he always kept in his front breast pocket.

I watched him for a few minutes as he tapped his pen against the paper, even though he was finished writing. "What's on your mind?"

"I was up at Stetson's Corner late last night." I groaned, already knowing that nothing good was going to come from this. If older ladies did their gossiping at Sheer Delights, the beauty parlor located between the feed store and ammo store, then the older men of the area did their gossiping up at Stetson's Corner. It wasn't anything special, just a convenience store and gas station, but they had a place to tie their horses so the men congregated. "There's a lot of talk about that town meeting. People say it ain't good. They think this man is going to ruin all of us."

"Don't buy into that. Whatever it is, I'm going to fight it, and if we end up having to move, we will. But you'll still have a job as long as you want it."

"Last time there was this much skuttlebutt was about

thirty years ago when the Smithsonian sent some scientists here and a whole bunch of reporters followed. They were trying to prove if one of the guys who conspired along with John Wilkes Booth to kill Abraham Lincoln was buried in the cemetery."

"Is one of the guys buried there?"

"Sure is."

I shook my head. "In this little town? What's our population, twelve?"

"Nah, thirteen now that London had that baby."

I laughed because I knew that, in all truthfulness, there was more like three thousand in our town. I stood there, waiting to see if he had anything else on his mind, but after a minute, it was clear that he didn't, so I moved on.

"Well, I've got some calls to make. Holland from next door is coming over and we're going to figure out if there is anything we can do. I'll let you know what we come up with, but I think that we're all going to be fine," I said as I left Slipper's stall and moved over to the small sink to wash my hands.

"I sure hope you're right."

"I have some office work to do today, so let me know if you need anything or if Noah needs help with the horses." I started walking toward the doors.

"Will do. By the way, we're getting low on protein," Syd called after me.

"Already on order. Delivery should be here tomorrow."

Back in my house, I moved to my office and called my attorney, Arthur Bankston.

"Thank you for calling the law offices of Bankston and Byrd. How may I help you?"

"This is Reid Brooks, I'm trying to reach Arthur Bankston please."

"One second please."

The line clicked, and then the horrific instrumental version of Lionel Richie's "All Night Long" hit my ear. Really? That song was never meant to have an instrumental musac version.

The music clicked off and my attorney's voice came over. "Reid, I hope that everything is okay?"

"Me, too, but I may need your help."

"Tell me how I can help you."

"I'm not sure where to even begin because I'm not suing anyone or at least I don't think I am." I dragged my thumbnail along the carved edge of my desk. It was always at times like this when you noticed shit caked in crevices, and it bothered the hell out of you until you picked at it.

"What's happened?"

"Last night, Johnson Holbrook told the town that we basically needed to sell him portions of our land . . ." I walked Arthur through the details of the eminent domain claim and how he professed that it was already settled and was doing us a favor by paying above what the state would.

"Let me look into this some more but it doesn't sound right. I've got some contacts up in Tallahassee that I'll get in touch with to see about the minutes from the Cabinet meetings as well as the Transportation Commission meetings. But from what I know about eminent domain, this is not how things work. Unfortunately Florida doesn't have clear laws concerning this except for the original constitution. But there are several precedents that are prevailing. Don't do anything, don't talk with him, don't sign anything, and tell the others not to either. I'll need a few days, but I will get back to you as soon as possible."

"Thanks, Arthur."

"No problem." We disconnected, and I spent the next several hours researching information about the town of Geneva, Florida, as well as eminent domain.

Just after three, Holland still hadn't showed, so I decided that I'd get dinner going just in case I convinced her to stay. What was I thinking? The woman was so insufferable she would probably show up tomorrow morning just to leave me hanging. Still, I found myself in the kitchen and started chopping vegetables.

"I thought that I told you I wouldn't be here tonight for dinner," my sister said as she came into the kitchen and examined the two New York strips that I had set out to defrost. Ellie had moved in with me a little over a year ago after her divorce, and probably wasn't leaving anytime soon.

"Yep, you told me." I reached into the refrigerator and grabbed the stuff to make a salad.

"Then why two steaks? Are you on some protein kick that I don't know about?"

"Holland is coming over."

Ellie started pounding her chest and coughing. "Uh-uh, Holland? As in our next door neighbor Holland Kelly, the one that would rather run you over than look at you? The Holland who I have yet to hear call you by anything other than Dick Brooks, that Holland?"

"Yep."

"And you think serving food that require knives to cut is a good idea?"

I stopped pulling apart the lettuce. "Maybe I didn't think this one out totally."

"You think?" Ellie picked up her purse. "Well, if there's blood everywhere when I get home, at least you can't say that I didn't warn you. I'm headed up to help Marcus, he's down a waitress, so I offered to help."

"Who are you? First you decided to start a mobile dog grooming business, and now you're serving drinks in a country dive bar? If our parents saw you—"

"What? They wouldn't do anything more than lecture me

about how I'm better than that. 'You are Ellis Brooks, and Brooks do not wait on people.'" Ellie's accent of our mother was spot on. "I've always hated it when she used my full name." Our mother was raised on Southern money and believed girls should be debutantes, which was why she'd named my sister Ellis. I was just glad Ellie didn't live up to the pretentiousness of it.

"Go. I think I can handle Holland."

Ellie patted my arm. "Just keep telling yourself that." She walked out of the house laughing.

Chapter Four

HOLLAND

It was like pulling teeth—no, that was painful but didn't last that long. This was more like ripping a nail down to the quick and then constantly hitting it against things. Yeah, that was more like it. It was a constant pain. I didn't know how else to describe knowing that I was going to come face-to-face with Reid Brooks in a matter of moments.

I steeled myself, ready for combat as I trudged up the few steps to his oversized house. It really was ridiculous, especially when you realized he had all seven thousand square feet to himself when he bought the place.

I raised one hand to knock, but before I could, the door swung open. "Holland, you came."

"I said I would, didn't I?"

"Yes, but let's be honest, you do go out of your way to inconvenience me."

"Well, this time I'm going out of my way to make you miserable. I decided to actually show up."

He smiled and stepped back so I could walk inside.

"I need to check a few things in the stables, why don't you walk with me?"

I wanted to say something snappy, but the truth was I was curious as hell to see his stables. "Yeah, we can do that. Do you only have Thoroughbreds? I don't know much about them."

"Yeah, all of them but my horse are."

"Oh, yeah, a Fresian, right?"

"Very good, yeah. Nostradamus." Reid grabbed a clipboard and scanned what appeared to be X-rays.

"Is someone hurt?"

"Yeah, Slipper." He gestured to a stall toward the back. "She fractured her cannon bone."

"Ouch."

"Tell me about it."

"Do you mind if I look?"

"Not at all. I'd like to hear your take on it."

He wanted my opinion? "Umm, well . . . I'm assuming she won't race anymore, but for European or Western riding, she should be okay, right?"

"I would say that's best. At least that is what I would do but I'm not the owner," Reid said as he handed me the X-rays.

"I've never seen that film, it almost has a chalky feel to it, did Asher take these?"

"No, we have our own machine. Since so many of the horses come here to heal and regain strength after an injury, it only made sense to have our own. That way we could monitor the healing process. Not to mention, some of these horses are worth more than my house."

"Why Thoroughbreds? I mean, they're beautiful and all, but around here, we have more Appaloosas and Quarter Horses. You don't ride Thoroughbreds just for the hell of it."

"Thoroughbreds are what I know. In fact, I moved to Florida with the sole purpose of setting up a stable where people I knew could bring their horses for the winter. Most owners and breeders shuttle their horses to warmer climates during the cold months to avoid any flare-ups of arthritis."

"And you know enough people who work with horses to do that?"

"I do. I was raised in Lexington, and my father is a breeder of Thoroughbreds, several of which have run in the Derby—we've even had a winner. People trust my family, so when I let everyone know that I was opening a winter stable, they scrambled for a spot." Reid explained this as he moved into the stall he'd gestured to a moment ago. He knelt by her and rubbed her wrapped leg.

"Is that why you named it Old Kentucky?"

"That, and because it's the name of my family's stables back home."

"But don't you want to run your family's stables someday?"

"That'll never happen."

"Why not?"

"I have two older brothers. They're also into Thoroughbreds. My eldest brother, Adler, actually runs the stables, and Cooper is a large animal veterinarian who only treats race horses."

"Reid, Adler, and Cooper? Sounds like a law firm if you ask me." I bit my lower lip and fought the urge to laugh.

"Don't forget Ellie, whose real name is Ellis, and we have an older sister named Lennon."

"Those are unique names."

Reid raised one brow. "Really, Holland? And your sisters are London and Paris?"

"Touché."

"My family has this thing about giving last names as first names. My grandmother's maiden name was Lennon, and Ellis got my mother's maiden name."

"How about the boys, where did those names come from?"

"They come from grandmothers and great-grandmothers as far back as they want to go." Reid smiled, appearing pleased with whatever he saw with Slipper as he stood. "Let me turn off the lights and we can head up to the house. I put two steaks on the smoker, they should be ready by the time we get up there."

"I said no to dinner."

"Stop being an ass, it is after six. Let's eat, and we can make a plan." I wanted to get pissed, but of course, my stomach let out a gurgling sound. "Fine," I huffed. Reid closed up and then he and I walked up to his house. It was weird, but I had enjoyed talking with Reid and getting to know him.

After eating, we moved into Reid's sunroom, and I looked for some sign that I was being punked. There was no way I was relaxed and not on high alert waiting for him to take some pot shot at me. He and I had been enemies for two years, but damn it all, I was comfortable.

I was sitting on one of his oversized chairs with one leg hiked up on the seat with me. "So, let's talk plan. I've done some research, how about you?"

"I have, too, and I put a call into my attorney today."

"Does he handle eminent domain?"

"He handles land deals, worked with me to make sure the zoning was correct when I bought this property."

"Well, we may not need him. Did you know that in 2006, President Bush issued an executive order limiting the use of taking private property for public use?" I slid my foot back to the floor and sat a little straighter. "It nearly eradicated the use of eminent domain. And the few times that it has been evoked since then, it has only used federal money, not private money." I knew that my hands were flying in sync with my words, but I had so much to say and I wanted to get it all out as quick as I could.

"Slow down there, Tiger. With the way you're flapping your arms, if you aren't careful, then you're gonna fly off."

I slapped my hands down to my sides. Fuck him, how dare he make fun of me. "I was just trying to find information to help all of us, and you're making fun of me."

"I'm not making fun of you, I'm teasing. Holy shit, Holland, learn to take a joke. Anyway, let's get back to why we are here. I personally think Johnson Holbrook is full of shit and that we aren't at risk of eminent domain at all."

"That's awesome, then why am I here? Why don't you tell him to kiss our asses, get the hell out of dodge, and stop wasting our time?"

"Because I want to know what it is he wants. There has to be something, some reason this man is willing to try to buy all of these randomly placed pieces of land."

"Then, do you care to tell me why you believe we aren't at risk? Granted, from what I can see, some of the parcels aren't big enough to ranch or farm on and some don't even meet the minimum five acre rule for housing."

"Not just that, they also aren't connected. Have you ever watched a road crew? They spread out, and it seems to me like a road this large would go over a lot more property because he can build it over people's homes. When you buy land, you also buy the space straight up, hell, they can't even put telephone lines across land unless it is part of the easement."

"Do they even install above ground phone lines anymore?"

"You know what I mean. But this is why I haven't told him to fuck off yet." Reid slid one hand down his face. He looked tired, and the skin under his blue eyes appeared bruised.

"What could he be after that would involve the councilman if it isn't official business?"

"That's what we need to find out if we can."

Reid scratched the side of his neck, and it drew my attention to the way his muscles flexed. For the first time, I truly noticed how sculpted the man's biceps were. I may not understand Thoroughbreds, but Thoroughbreds had done a body good. I couldn't take my eyes off the way the veins in his hands were raised and only made him look more masculine. I wondered what his would feel like gripping—

A hand waved in front of my face. "Holland, you okay? Holland?"

"What?"

"I asked if you were okay?"

"Yeah, why?"

"You were staring at me, at first I thought that you were pissed at something, then I was afraid you were having some sort of seizure. You sure you're okay?"

"Yeah." I felt my cheeks warm. "I think looking into the councilman is a good start."

"Wow, okay, you really missed a lot. From my understanding the Geneva Cemetery is historic, so I want to talk with the historical society and see what else we can uncover. If Holbrook is trying to build here, history will keep any builder away." Reid paused for a moment and pinched his lips as if he were trying to think through something.

"What?"

"Cemeteries can be moved. We need more."

"There are some civil war soldiers buried in the cemetery, will that help?"

"Those can be relocated."

"Umm, Chief Osceola used to live here."

"Seminole Chief, that Osceola?"

"Yeah, he had a village somewhere on Lake Harney so it could have been any of our properties. That also means he has to have hunted through the woods here."

"This is perfect. Have they deemed any areas as Native American burial grounds?"

"Not that I know of, but we could always ask the historical society what they know. So, is that part of the plan, we're trying to get on a National Registry?" I grabbed my notebook, the one I had written Google discoveries in, and was ready to take more notes.

"I don't know. We just need enough to cause a stir, which will hopefully stall him so that we can figure out what's going on."

"You truly think he made all of this up?"

"I'm not sure yet. He's either trying to jump the gun to ensure he gets the contract or he's using it as an excuse to bully the landowners. I do know that Johnson Holbrook develops subdivisions and luxury homes, but I haven't found one single record of where he's been involved with road development."

"That sorry son of a bitch."

"That's one way of putting it." Reid glanced over at me. "Will you go to the historical society to see what you can dig up?"

I let out a loud groan. "Ugh, that place is so boring."

"I'll take that as a yes. After you talk to them, I'd like us to meet with the ranchers. I want to make sure that Holbrook doesn't persuade any of them—"

"You mean bully." I had no clue why Reid was trying to soften the truth because that man was going to use whatever he could to get our land and had already proven he wasn't above intimidation.

"Okay, bully."

"Why don't you just schedule a meeting with the ranchers? They trust you more than they do me."

"I wouldn't be so sure about that. They listen to what I have to say as a businessman, but their decisions are based on what is best for you and your sisters. This town, these people love you."

Reid turned thoughtful, and I let him ponder his plan as I looked out the wall-to-wall windows that overlooked the back of his property. To the right, it gave a beautiful view of my training area, where I taught riding classes. I smiled because it also gave a good view of our stables, which really were beautiful. They were more rustic than Reid's but equally as breathtaking. A light in the dormer window—crap, that was my room. I wondered if Reid knew that was my room or if he saw me flip him off every day.

"I better go. I'll talk to the historical society. You see what your attorney can find out. Do we know anyone who might have information about proposed road improvements and new extensions?"

"I'm working on it. There's an investigator who my brother used a few years back, they were having issues with an owner stacking the books."

"What does that mean?"

"It means that the owner had a great horse but would force the jockey to lose several races so that odds were against them. Then when the stakes were high, he'd have him go full throttle for the win and take the purse."

"And the investigator caught him?"

Reid nodded. "Yep, got us everything Adler needed to take to the racing commission and get the owner permanently banned. Anyway, I want to see if I can hire the investigator he used to work this case."

I tapped my pen against my notepad and then flipped to a clean sheet. "So, we are dividing and conquering. Your attorney is checking on what?"

"Laws about eminent domain and contacting the Transportation Commission."

"I'm going to the historical society, and you are contacting some guy who is going to get the lowdown on Holbrook?"

"And possibly Shane," Reid reminded me.

"Yeah, possibly the councilman." I stood and glanced to the clock before making my way to the door. Reid followed just close enough behind me that I couldn't ignore his presence.

"Holland?"

"Yes?" I said without turning to look at him. I kind of just needed to get out of his house.

"I liked not fighting with you tonight."

His words made me uncomfortable, so I pulled my indifference around me like a damn coat. "Don't get used to it."

Reid let out a loud chuckle. "Why am I not surprised?" I flipped him off and headed out the back door.

Chapter Five

REID

Why was it that it was easy to get out bed at five some mornings, but other mornings it seemed as if the world would end if I opened my eyes? Oh, I knew. It was because the latter were usually the mornings after I'd stayed up too late thinking about Holland.

After heaving myself out of bed, I headed to the kitchen. I needed coffee and lots of it. Once I had a nice tall Yeti cup full in one hand, I grabbed my phone with the other. There were few people who I knew that I could call at this time of the morning but as I scrolled through my contacts and stopped on my oldest brother's name, he was one of them.

"Hey, what's up?" Adler asked as way of answering.

"I didn't wake you, did I?"

"Ha ha, just sitting at the table and finishing breakfast."

"You have a second?"

"Sure, do I need to go into the other room? Elizabeth is sitting by me."

"No. Tell her I said good morning and I'm sorry for interrupting y'all's time together." I listened as Adler repeated my message to her. "She says good morning as well. Now tell me what's going on."

"Hey, I'm having some problems with a dirty business-man. I was calling to see if I could get the contact informa-tion for the private investigator you hired a few years back?"

My brother paused for several seconds, which was some-thing out of the norm for him. He was usually so self-confi-dent. "It wasn't a he; it was a she."

"I don't care about that. I just want someone who is good and can dig up dirt."

"Yeah, well . . ."

"What, Adler? What the fuck aren't you telling me?"

"It was Brandy, Brandy Lakote." I let out a long whistle. "Yeah, I know, that's why I never told you the name. Look, we didn't know it was her until after we had called the company. She came highly recommended. She was certified nationwide, which was what we needed since races were in different states." My brother kept babbling on but I hadn't said a word.

Brandy Lakote had been my high-school sweetheart. One date with her, and I was a goner. I thought she was the one. For two years, I spent every day and night thanking the good Lord that she was on my arm. But I got a football scholarship to UK and she wanted to go to school in Texas. We broke it off, promising to still be friends. I let out a half-chuckle, half-groan because those things never happened, people never remained friends. And I never heard from Brandy again. At that time, I thought I was going to die.

"Reid? Are you there?"

"Yeah, sorry."

"She's good. She is a computer genius and has a way with words, I think that she could talk the devil into changing his ways."

"She always had a way with words."

"I'm sorry, man."

"No need. Water under the bridge." My family knew all too well the heartbreak I had suffered, looking back it seemed like just a stepping-stone. Something I needed to go through to be me. "Do you have her number handy?"

"Sure, but what's going on, what kind of dirty businessman?"

"There's a land developer threatening eminent domain, but he's bullying people about it. I want to find out what he's really doing."

"What I know about eminent domain is that it takes a while, there will be lots of hearings, and it will all make sense. Maybe not to the people losing their land, but if you step back, you can see how it is all connected."

"That's the problem, there haven't been hearings, and the first time anyone heard about it was at that meeting. For some reason, this developer has a councilman on his side. As far as the land, it's random pieces that don't make sense for what they are proposing."

"If there's something shady going on Brandy will find it. You got a pen handy?" Adler asked.

"Yep." I grabbed one from the junk drawer as Adler called off her number.

"That's her cell. She travels all over so I found that calling around noon our time was best. Just in case she was on the west coast or something then I wasn't calling too early."

"Thanks. I'll call her later." I disconnected and then entered her number into my phone's contacts. Before folding the piece of paper in half, I stared down at it, a memory of when she had given me her number on a piece of torn notebook paper flashed in front of my eyes. Shaking my head, I stuck the note on my fridge with a magnet as backup.

Then I got ready for my day and headed down to the stables. My mind was still on how to approach Brandy, when I heard the rumble of tires and looked to see one particular truck leaving the Kelly Ranch. Of course, it was flying like a bat out of hell. Holland Rose Kelly . . . fast at everything . . . driving, riding, and let's not forget losing her temper.

Chapter Six

HOLLAND

This was the definition of purgatory. Yeah, it wasn't hell because I could imagine things being worse but I couldn't imagine anything being more boring. I was sitting at a long oak table that had been hand carved, I know this because I had been told no less than nine times by Miss Nancy, the town historian. Oh, and it was hand carved by Mrs. Yarborough's great-grandfather. And just in case you're wondering, Mrs. Yarborough's sister ran off with a door-to-door salesman. Not interested? That was okay, neither was I, nor was I interested in hearing about the Buckland family who still resided in these parts or the Slaviks, who moved away in nineteen thirty, but not to worry because their grandchildren still lived here.

The historian was in her late seventies and wore clothes that were obviously from the late seventies as well: a plaid short sleeve shirt with pearl snaps and puffed sleeves tucked into the mom version of bell-bottom jeans that rested under her boobs. It was set off by beauty parlor permed gray hair.

"Miss Nancy . . ."

"And we have an old Edison record player. Here, let me play it for you." Miss Nancy got up and slid a long tube onto the player. "This record player doesn't have electricity, so the needle doesn't move. See the record? It isn't round like you kids are used to." I decided that I probably shouldn't tell her that records were before my time as well. "I have to crank it to get it playing."

"That's an interesting piece of history." I gave her a tight smile and waited just long enough to avoid coming across as rude before saying, "I really stopped by to talk you about something, though."

"Oh, why didn't you say so?"

Umm, I did, several times. As she walked past items, I could tell that she was longing to tell me about them, and part of me felt bad for stopping her, but I had to get back to the ranch, I had chores to do.

"I was wondering if you knew anything about historical events that happened in Geneva. Maybe about historically important people who have lived here or died here?"

"Well, Chief Osceola . . ." Miss Nancy began her long history of who, when, where, and even why people had moved in and out of Geneva. "The Anthropological Society discovered shards of pottery from 1450 BC—"

"BC as in before Christ?"

"Yes, ma'am, the Timucuan Indians called this area home. And there are maps that show William Powell, who most people know as Chief Osceola had a village here in 1835 . . ."

I wrote down each fact, including the one about the two acres of Indian burial grounds. When Miss Nancy was finally finished, I pushed my chair back before she began on another history lesson. "Thank you so much for your time. If I have more questions, may I call you?"

"Absolutely. Let me give you one of the cards." She handed

me a pamphlet with the address and number of the museum, which wasn't exactly a business card, but I smiled anyway.

"Thank you again," I said as I tucked everything into my bag before heading home.

When I pulled into my driveway, there was a shiny Ford F-250 Platinum Super Crew cab parked in front of my house. Yeah, I knew my pickup trucks. I also knew that there was no way in hell I would be willing to spend almost ninety thousand for one.

What I didn't know was who owned that truck or why it was at my house.

When I walked inside, Paris was in the kitchen, and she turned to me with a smile. "Hey, you're back."

"I am, but I never thought I was getting out of there. Who is overcompensating for the lack of something?"

"What do you mean?"

"I think she's referring to me."

I turned and grimaced. "Should have known. What are you doing here?" Johnson Holbrook was standing in my home, and all I could think was: where the hell had we put Daddy's gun.

"Waiting for you. Seems your sisters refuse to talk to me as well."

"Seems my sisters have good judgment."

"I had him wait in my office until you came back since I had work to do and no time to babysit. Plus, he refused to believe that I wasn't you," London said. The three of us were almost identical, and if it weren't for each of us being three years apart, we could have told people we were triplets.

"What do you want, Mr. Holbrook?"

"Well, young lady, I was hoping that I might have a moment of your time. It seems that we got off on the wrong foot."

"You think? Was it the part where you told everyone that it was small pieces of land and then I find out it is twenty-five percent of ours or was it the part where you told me that you didn't have to pay us your elevated"—I used air quotes when I said *elevated*—"price. Or, wait I've got it, not to get on your bad side. Let me ask you, Mr. Holbrook, do you have a good side?"

As I waited for him to say something back to me, I took in him in. He was trying hard to fit in . . . too hard. His John Deere shirt was crisp and new. He had obviously gone and raided Tractor Supply along with his brand new, not broken in, had to be killing him and giving him blisters, Lucchese cowboy boots. When he didn't say anything, I decided to keep prodding, of course I did. I knew that my temper was my downfall but damn it all to hell, I needed an outlet. "Fancy boots." I smirked. Those things set him back a good thousand dollars or more, and for what? To impress a bunch of people who couldn't care less about brand names.

"I'm a businessman, but I'm also a family man. I understand that you love this land because it has been in your family."

"You could say that. My grandfather grew up on this property, and my dad was born in this house."

"And now both of your sisters have homes here and are building their own families here. That's why I went to the surveyors to see if we could try to salvage some of your land. I know that originally we were asking for one-hundred acres." Holbrook reached into what could only be an ostrich leather briefcase and pulled out folded papers. "If you see here, it looks as if we can get by with seventy-one acres. I know that still sounds like a lot, but it is better . . . don't you think?"

"Much better," Paris added. "It looks as if it is toward the back, so the stables would stay." I cut my eyes to Paris and gave her a silent but no less effective shut-the-hell-up stare.

"See, I'm a reasonable guy." He grabbed another form and a pen. "Let's save us both the headache and take care of all of this right now. I've upped the offer per acre a substantial amount."

I took the paper and pen and read over it, he had raised the offer by almost two hundred dollars per acre. "Wow, you must really want this property if you're willing to pay this much, it does give one reason to pause. I have to ask myself . . . why?" I touched the pen to the paper, and in one swift movement wrote, *hell no,* from top corner to bottom corner. Then recapped the pen and handed them both back over. "Thanks for stopping by, but I think that you're full of shit and right now the only thing I have time for is horse shit, got to go clean the stables and shovel some."

He shook his head at me. "Well, I came to let you know that several of your neighbors have agreed to sell." I closed my eyes and took a few deep breaths. I was glad that my back was to him. Reid and I needed to get to the ranchers and talk with them—like now. At least, we needed to talk to the ones who hadn't agreed to sell yet.

"There's no sense holding out, Miss Kelly. We're moving forward with this deal, and it would be nice to have you on board, but it isn't necessary. Especially since Reid Brooks just agreed to sell us less acres for more money."

"Reid Brooks is selling his property? You have his signature on your contracts?"

"Sure do. It was a mutual agreement that we would not go after more of his land."

I couldn't believe Reid was selling. No way, he wouldn't, he couldn't. If he did? Just wait until I get my hands around that two-faced, no-good, son-of-a-bitch's neck. And let's be honest, it will be sad not having him around to aggravate or gaze upon, he was rather attractive.

He reached into his briefcase, pulled out a Manila envelope, and held it out to me. "I'll give you one more chance. Miss Kelly, I advise you to take this offer. It isn't going to be this good again."

I took the envelope. "Well, if it is written in these papers, then at least I know it can't get any worse, right? If everything you're promising me isn't in the papers, then why would I sign in the first place?" I smiled when my statement squashed his empty threat. Yeah, that was right, city slicker, I might not be the brightest crayon in the box, but I sure as hell wasn't as dull as you. Or Dick Brooks, for that matter. "Thank you for bringing these out." I stood and resisted the urge to shove the envelope into the garbage disposal. "Let me see you to the door."

"Listen—"

I held up a hand. "No, I've heard what you have to say, and now it's time for you to go. I'll look these over and talk with an attorney. If you change your mind about your offer in the meantime, we will take it as a sign that you are not the kind of person we want to do business with. It will be proof that we will need to fight you and this so-called eminent domain. If that is truly coming down the pipeline."

"Oh, it is, little lady."

"Yeah, still a condescending asshole, that isn't winning you any favors." I opened my front door and waved one arm, signaling for him to get the hell out of my house. When he finally did, I slammed it shut and turned to face my sisters.

"This is exactly why I wanted you to deal with him. You stand strong, he tried to rile you, but you didn't get into a pissing match over whether or not Reid agreed to sell." London folded her arms and leaned against the doorframe of her office.

"No joke. He was pissed that he couldn't force you to be a biddable *young lady*." Paris was stirring something in a large bowl that she had cradled in the crook of one arm.

"I'm not so sure about that. But I do need to talk with dickhead next door."

"Do me a favor?" Paris asked.

"What's that?"

"Calm down first. Go do your normal work and give your-self time to think before you go."

"Okay."

"Promise?" London raised one eyebrow, totally not believing my word. "You don't know that he's selling. This Holbrook fellow may be lying about that as well."

Throwing my hands up in the air, I headed out the door and heard them laughing behind me as I walked to the stables. When I got inside and got to mucking out the stalls, it had the opposite effect on me. Instead of calming me, it ignited my inner fire.

Ugh, I hated Johnson Holbrook. He was a giant douche canoe. A dickcicle. I used the pitchfork to shovel the dirty hay into the wheelbarrow and then add fresh to the first stall, which was Ursula's, and then I moved down to the next. There was no way on God's green earth that Reid would sell, Holbrook was lying. Reid and I were a team. We were working together. I moved on to the next stall. I was just going to have to go over there and ask Reid myself. Hell, he had hired an attorney. There wasn't any way he would sell. We made a plan of attack . . . together. Crap, I wasn't going to get one moment of peace until I asked him.

I marched over to the fence that separated our two stables, be nice, be polite, I kept chanting to myself. "Brooks. Hey, Reid, I have a question for you!" I shouted loud enough so he could hear me.

He came out of the side of his barn nearest me, and I smiled brightly. "What's up?"

"Did you tell Holbrook that you would sell?"

"Yep, but I have—"

I didn't waste one more second on him or what he had to say. I flipped him off then stalked back to my stables and got back to work. The horses sensed my stress, and they started moving around their stalls and kicking at the walls.

With each stab of my pitchfork to rotate hay, I envisioned Reid smiling as if he thought that he'd gotten the upper hand. Upper hand on what, I had no idea, but the upper hand nonetheless. When I grabbed the wheelbarrow full of manure, I totally intended to take it to the compost pile, I did . . . really, but something came over me.

Rolling the cart out of the backside of the stables and toward Reid's house, I pushed it along the fence until I was parallel with his sunroom. Then I grabbed a handful of manure and pressed it into a ball. I packed it good and tight, pulled my arm back like I was the starting pitcher for the New York Yankees, and let it fly.

It hit the side of his house with a very satisfying *smack*.

"Home run!" I shouted as I ran around the wheelbarrow, my arms in the air. Coming back to what I had deemed home plate, I packed another shit-ball. In my best announcer voice, "Holland Kelly is warmed up, the fans are on their feet, the bases loaded, and she lets it fly." I tossed it, and it smacked against the house. "And that, my friends, is what we call a grand slam-slam-slam . . ." I added the echo that always seemed to appear in epic baseball movies.

"Holland Kelly, what the hell do you think you're doing?" I looked to my left and saw Reid walking toward me with his hands on his hips.

What was I doing? Well, I was making another ball. When I was done, I held it up. "Don't take another step." I waved it in the air.

"What the hell? Have you lost your mind?"

My anger was raging inside me, I couldn't control it, I let

the manure fly. "All your words about helping, making a plan, were what? Nothing! You are nothing but a liar, and I hate you, Dick Brooks!"

Chapter Seven

REID

I wasn't sure exactly what had gotten into her, but I knew that it was only a matter of seconds before I would be covered in horse shit if I didn't do something. When she threw the ball at me, I cut right, and she missed.

"Dick Brooks!" she yelled as she bent over and scooped up another handful.

"Stop, damn it, will you just stop?" I shouted as I vaulted over the fence separating us and made my way to her.

"No, I will not. You made me think that you just might be a good guy. You aren't." She threw another handful, and I ducked. When she bent to scoop more, I grabbed her by the waist and pulled her away from the wheelbarrow.

"Calm down, Tiger, and tell me what's wrong."

"You know damn well what's wrong. Let go of me." She squirmed, but I wasn't letting go.

"Keep it up, and I'll sit you in the wheelbarrow. Now tell me what's going on."

"You agreed to sell to that snake and have ruined everything. All I've ever wanted was to have the stables and teach riding. I dreamed of someday blocking off another two acres and teach barrel racing and now that is never going to happen and I'm going to lose everything!"

"You know how to do that? Barrel racing?"

"Yes. Don't sound so shocked. I'm actually good with horses."

"I know you're good." She stopped squirming. "It's more fun to give you a hard time."

"Is that why you did it, to give me a hard time, to make my life miserable?"

There was a vulnerability in her tone that I'd never heard before. "Why I did what? I have no clue what you're talking about." I set her down but still kept my arms around her.

She slid her gloves off and threw them to the ground. "Why you agreed to sell—"

"Wait. That is what this is about? If you had let me finish before you would have known that he asked me if I would sell less acres for more money. I said I would consider the offer, and he told me that he would be right over for me to sign the paperwork. I told him I wouldn't sign anything until my attorney got back to me with the information that I'd requested. He wanted to know what information that was, and I told him to be patient."

Holland looked over her shoulder, allowing me to see the tears in her amber-colored eyes. "So, you didn't sign?"

"No, and I'm a bit upset that you would believe anything that man would say. You have to know that I wouldn't do that to you. We are in this together, remember? I'm not going to let some developer come in and destroy your stables and build a highway on top of our properties. If they did that, it would tank our property values."

She let out a burst of laughter. "See, I knew there was an ulterior motive."

"Well, I was thinking of the horses, too. All the noises would keep the horses so spooked that I doubt any of them would train." I released my hold on her, and she slowly turned around. "I wouldn't do that to you. I don't break my word . . . ever."

"I'm so afraid that I'm going to lose everything. Those stables are all I have left of my dad. He built them for me. Sure, they belong to the three of us, but it was for me." A tear ran down her cheek.

She was so beautiful and so open and honest in that moment, that I couldn't seem to stop myself from stepping forward and sliding my hand to the back of her neck. My lips were crashing down on hers, and she was pressing closer to me.

The smallest of moans slipped from her, and that was it. There was no stopping whatever it was that had come over me—dementia, madness, hysteria, I wasn't sure, but whatever it was, I had no intention of stopping.

My tongue tangled with hers, which earned me more of those tiny moans that made me want to rip her clothes off. My hand found its way into the back of her hair, and I held her closer.

When she wrapped her arms around my waist, I'd forgotten that we were standing in the open so anyone could see us or that just a few minutes ago she'd been angry and throwing manure at my house. No, I had one thing on my mind, and that was how I was going to get Holland into my house and up to my room the fastest.

I wasn't sure if I had somehow pulled away during my thoughts of her in my room or if she had felt my hard cock pressed against her and freaked out, but in the next moment, there were three feet between us and we were both breathing heavily.

"What did you do that for, Reid?"

"Probably for the same reason you were doing it to me."

Holland blanched and swiped her fingertips across her

swollen lips before glaring and flipping me off. "Don't ever do that again. Next time, you should ask a lady before you assume that she wants to be kissed." I let out a loud chuckle. "Don't laugh at me." Her anger only made me laugh harder. "Stop it. Damn you." Holland bent and scooped her gloves up.

"Oh, no, you don't." I grabbed her. "You do it again, and I'm carrying you up to my house and showing you what kissing is really like. Now, calm down. You still need to clean the side of my house."

"Screw you, Reid Brooks."

"Is that an offer, Holland?"

She scoffed and then turned without bothering to take her wheelbarrow with her. I stood there, watching the angry sway of her hips as she walked off, imagining what she would look like bent over the foot of my bed. The daydream was so vivid that I almost missed it when she stopped and flipped me off again.

Almost.

God, I had no clue what Holland Kelly was doing to me but I sure as hell wanted to find out.

———

I imagined long blonde hair bouncing with the rhythm of the horse's gait. Eyes the color of whiskey, and the burn from the first swallow matching the temper of the woman. Fuck, ever since kissing her, she was all that I could think about.

My phone rang, so I set aside my sketchpad and charcoal and answered it, "Hello?"

"Hey, Reid, it's Marcus."

"What's up?"

"Just wanted to give you a heads-up." I groaned, worried

that he was calling to bitch me out about Holland but hoping that it was something else . . . anything else.

"Yeah?"

"You know that land guy who's been bugging the hell out of everyone?"

"Yes?" I take it back. I'd rather this be about Holland.

"Well, he's up here with Mr. Brown, Mr. Kirby, and a few others. He has a tab going and putting their drinks on it."

"Son of a bitch. He's trying to buy his way into their favor. I'll be up in a few, but can you keep an ear on them for me?"

"Sure will."

"Thanks, man."

Ten minutes later, I was walking into the Elbow Room and heading toward the bar

"Hey, Marcus, a Yuengl—" My request was cut off by an ice-cold beer being set in front of me, he'd already read my mind. "Thanks. Where is he?"

"No problem." He darted his eyes to the side, making sure that I saw the group in the back corner of the bar. "From what I've heard, he's been keeping the conversation light, probably trying to make them think he's a good ol' boy or some shit."

"Makes sense. He wants them to drop their guards and think he's a friend." I leaned back on my stool, turning the bottle around as if I couldn't keep my hands still. "I'm going to go remind them that he is not a friend to any of us."

"Good luck."

I nodded and brought my drink with me when I made my way over to the group.

"Is this a private meeting or is anyone invited?"

"Private," Holbrook said, and I smirked as I pulled out a seat.

"Since he's selling, I think he should be here," Mr. Brown

said, which was something Holbrook clearly didn't appreciate.

"I'm what? Where did you hear a rumor like that?" The ranchers all turned their glances to Holbrook. I would have thought the asshole would slink down into his chair a bit, but he didn't. He actually sat straighter and puffed out his chest. He looked ridiculous.

"Mr. Brooks and I have already gone over all of this. This is your time to ask me questions. So, Mr. Brooks, if you'll excuse us."

"Okay," I said, and just as Holbrook looked relieved that I was leaving so easily, I turned to Mr. Brown and added, "Just one thing before I go. If he's telling you that I'm selling, then he's already lying to you. I flat out told him that I would *consider* his offer and was waiting to hear back from my attorney before I made any decisions, isn't that right, Mr. Holbrook?" I paused, putting him on the spot.

"You told us that he signed two days ago," Mr. Kirby announced.

"Well . . . I may have been misinformed, so I'll check on this and get back to you." Holbrook pushed back his chair.

"Oh, good. Since you're all done here, you wouldn't mind having a word with me in private, would you?" I asked before Holbrook got out of his seat.

Instead, the ranchers all pushed back from the table and stood.

"That lying snake," one man said as he walked off.

"Should've known better," someone, I think Mr. Brown, seethed while he headed for the door.

"I've had it with all this behind the back shit." I'm almost positive that was Mr. Kirby but I wasn't taking my eyes off Holbrook for one second to see who was actually speaking to be sure.

"Listen, I have to go; I have another appointment."

"No worries, this won't take long." I took a seat across from him and set my bottle in front of me, holding the base with both hands to keep from reaching forward and throat punching the asshole. "I don't care that you're a liar. Hell, I don't care that you lie about me. You couldn't actually hurt my business or me if you tried. What I do care about is you harassing my neighbors. Leave Holland Kelly alone."

"Or what? Her strip of property is the most important."

"And why is that?"

His silence in and of itself was telling since it let me know there was a reason. It just didn't tell me what the reason was.

"Fine. Play your games, but if you approach or attempt to coerce her into signing anything under duress, I will sue you for every single thing my lawyer can come up with."

"Don't threaten me, Reid, you won't like the consequences."

"Oh, that isn't a threat." I laughed. "That is a promise. Leave her alone or I'll have my attorney bury you in so many injunctions that you'll never see the sun again. Last I checked, neither the county nor the state did business deals with criminals."

The man had no clue the money I could get my hands on —hell, my grandparents on both sides had left me quite an inheritance that I had never touched. It had been sitting in mutual funds for years, just collecting compound interest. If I had to use it to protect what was mine, I would. That made me smile. Sometime in the last week, I'd claimed Holland Kelly as mine, and I really liked the thought.

I stood, glanced at Johnson Holbrook, and then decided that he wasn't worth anymore of my time. I headed back up to the bar where Marcus was working. "Another Yuengling, please."

"Please tell me that you have something to stop him?" Marcus asked as he set the new bottle in front of me.

"Yeah, I believe so. Hey, isn't your mom's property part of this?"

"Yes and I'm worried about her. I got the letter and haven't said anything, I'm her power of attorney anyway. But my mom is older, we don't know how much longer she has, and ever since Dad died, well . . . I think she is just about ready. This is all she knows, I'll do whatever you all need, I just don't want to see her lose her house."

"I seriously don't think that will happen, but I'll let you know as soon as we get some concrete information."

"We?"

"Yeah, Holland and I have been looking into it."

"Ah, and how is Holland? I don't suppose she's taking this mess that well."

"She threw horse manure at my house this morning when she thought I had sold my land to Holbrook."

Marcus burst into laughter and slapped his open palm against that bar. "Why does that not surprise me? That girl could never hold her temper."

"Tell me about it. She didn't even offer to hose it off after I told her that Holbrook had lied to her."

"You aren't going to do something like sell just to spite her, are you?"

What? "No, why would you ask that?"

"I only caught part of your conversation, but I heard her name. It's no secret the two of you aren't exactly friends, so you can understand that I had to ask. I like you, Reid, I do. But if it comes down to it, I'll side with the Kellys, and so will the town."

He probably meant that to be a warning, but it wasn't. I wouldn't do what he was suggesting and that was that. In spite of the feud Holland and I had, those girls had always garnered my respect. "She and I may argue, but I like arguing with her. I consider Holland a friend, and we *are* working together and trying to come up with a plan to stop this man. She just likes to grumble and bitch about stuff before she inevitably gives in. What you heard was me telling Holbrook to leave her alone or I'd have my attorney file a few hundred injunctions. He said that her property is the most important, and I think that he views her as weak because she's a woman."

"Holland? Weak?" Marcus smiled, and I grinned back. It really was a ludicrous thought.

"Exactly, the man is an idiot."

That was an ultimate low.

Not the kiss—that was great, too great. No, the flinging shit onto Reid's house was the ultimate low. After I had taken a shower, I sat in my apartment, staring out my dormer window and berating myself about the mess on the side of his house. I wanted to go over and clean it off, but my pride wouldn't let me. Knowing him, he would stand there and watch me clean every speck of it off and tell me how ashamed I should be for acting that way.

Yeah, I may be remorseful for doing it, but I wasn't *that* remorseful.

That was why, as soon as he pulled out of his driveway, I rushed over, jumped the fence, and headed for the hose coiled against the side of his house.

Of course, it didn't have a stupid nozzle on it, so I had to use my thumb to get the water pressure I needed.

"Ahhh, god, that's fucking freezing!" I shouted as icy cold water splayed in random directions, half of it hitting the wall I wanted it to hit and the other half hitting me and drenching my clothing.

I deserve this for letting my temper get the better of me.

I admonished myself but also acknowledged the fact that it wouldn't resonate with me. Nope, as soon as he pissed me off again, I would do something just as stupid. When his house was back to being white, I turned off the water and rolled the hose back up before heading back over the fence. I went to my stables and gathered the wheelbarrow and my gloves to finish my chores, dumping the contents into the compost pile.

I'd just stepped out of my second shower of the day when I noticed a blinking light on my phone. I'd missed a call from Marcus, which was weird since he never called me. I dialed him back.

"Hey, Holland."

"Sorry I missed your call. What's up?"

"I just wanted to let you know that Holbrook was up here with some of the ranchers and he was buying them drinks. I got ahold of Reid, and he came down to ruin the party."

I was glad to hear that Holbrook's plans were thwarted but pissed that Reid didn't come and get me.

"Anyway, there is something else I want to talk to you about, too."

"Okay, what?"

"Reid spoke to the guy alone."

"Okay." I wasn't sure why Marcus was calling to tell me this, but something in the pit of my stomach seemed to get heavy.

"He talked to him about you."

"About me? What did he say?" With my heart racing, I waited for Marcus's answer.

"He told Holbrook to leave you alone or he'd have his attorney file an injunction. Whatever Holbrook says? Don't believe him."

I wasn't sure how I felt about this, but that pit in my

stomach had lodged itself in my throat. "Thanks for the heads-up, Marcus, I appreciate it."

"Anytime. You know, all this time I thought the two of you hated each other, but after listening to Reid tonight, I'm not so sure."

"Wonders never cease, huh?"

"Yep, shocked the shit out of me. Talk to you later."

"Later."

I sat on my bed, peered out my window, and froze. The sight of that midnight blue Chevy Silverado had my heart racing again, but this time it felt totally different.

I wasn't sure how long I stared at it as I rubbed my hands back and forth along the old hand-sewn quilt that Mrs. Kinkaide, Marcus's mother, had made me when I was little. I rolled a piece of loose thread between my fingers and tried to come to grips with how I felt in that moment.

I wasn't sure how to explain it. It was just . . . I didn't know . . . different? I didn't hate Dick—maybe I should get into the habit of calling him Reid. It wasn't that I hated Reid. I knew I didn't. But did I like him? More importantly did I want him to like me?

I was still trying to ponder it out when footsteps started up the back stairs to my apartment. There were two ways to get into my apartment, one was from my kitchen area that led down to the stables, which were already locked up for the night, and the other set led from my tiny living room to the side parking area, which was the set that almost no one used.

I was up and out of bed before the footsteps made it to the top landing, and I peered out the window just as Reid Brooks raised his hand to knock. Not thinking, I flipped on the outside lights, and he squinted and shielded his eyes. *Shit.* I flipped them back off. The poor guy was probably blind.

"Damn it, Holland, you're going to fucking kill me. Open this damn door."

I did as he demanded and gave him an apologetic smile. "Yes?"

"May I come in?" He sounded exasperated. I took a step back and let him in. "Next time, don't flip so many lights on all at once and definitely don't plunge someone into pitch darkness immediately after. You nearly made me fall ass-backward down the steps."

I bit my lower lip and fought back the urge to grin. "I'm sorry."

"No, you aren't."

He was right. Although, had he fallen, I would have been. I was always remorseful. "What brings you by?"

He looked around my apartment, and I knew that he was judging me. My whole apartment could fit inside his living room. My place wasn't fancy, but it was clean, so I wasn't sure why it seemed as if he was trying not to touch anything. Hello, I always made my bed, and I couldn't go to sleep with a dirty dish in my sink, which wasn't really an issue since I ate most meals up at the big house.

"Are these all of you?" He walked over to large photos hanging on the walls. Okay, maybe he shouldn't grab a white glove or anything, I was not certain about the last time I dusted around my photo frames.

"Yep. My daddy used to buy all the pictures from my competitions. There were always photographers at the arenas to snap a photo of the riders while they were jumping, racing, or roping. When they saw Samuel Kelly, they saw the word *sucker* written on his forehead. He bought every damn photo. Then he would have several framed."

"They're beautiful. You look happy."

"I loved it. That's what I would do every day if I could. I'd ride and teach other people to ride Western."

"Then why don't you?"

"Not enough time in the day. Not enough space to setup.

I need a few more acres to build the right kind of training area so that the horses can truly practice and the riders have plenty of space to learn until they get used to cutting tight corners around barrels."

"You should be doing this, the look on your face . . . I understand why your dad bought all the photos." Reid continued examining the pictures. "What would you do with your stables if you had carte blanche ?"

"Why? You're all proper, I'm Western. We are so different, and you probably will think it is stupid." I was avoiding his question, but opening up about my dreams somehow made me feel like he was going to judge me or think I was stupid or childish for wanting them.

"I want to learn more about you, you know my dream, I'm living it—I always wanted to have my own stables. Tell me more about what you would do and how you would set it up."

"I'd build a few loading pins on the back of the stables and then make a giant arena where the horses could run around. It would take up the space where I currently have the paddock so I would have to build a new paddock. Then on the outside of the ring, I'd want some nice wooden benches so the parents could sit and watch if they wanted to. Although I could teach cutting and roping since we have cattle that isn't really my focus. I want to work on reining, trail riding, and barrel racing. There are several competitions around the state."

"I love how your eyes light up whenever you talk about horses and what you want to do." Reid tucked my hair behind one ear.

"Is this why you came over? To talk about my glory days of horse riding?"

"Umm, no." He took a seat on one of the two recliners in my living room and gestured for me to join him. "I came over to thank you for cleaning up the mess on my house."

"It was only fair, I caused it."

He nodded. "I also wanted to tell you that I went up to the Elbow Room tonight and Holbrook was there with Mr. Brown, Kirby, and a few others. He told them the same thing he told you, that I had agreed to sell."

"You clocked him, didn't you?"

"I wanted to, but no, I didn't. I did set them all straight, though."

"Good." Interesting that he didn't seem to want to tell me that he'd threatened Holbrook on my behalf.

"We need that meeting to be sooner rather than later. I originally thought that, once we got some concrete information, we could go to the other ranchers, but now I'm thinking we need to let them know what we're working on."

"I agree. No one likes to be left in the dark." Reid raised one eyebrow. "No. I swear I didn't mean to try to kill you." Reid smirked. "Okay, I didn't mean to try to kill you this time." I let out a laugh, and he joined me.

"You're a shit."

"I really am." I bit my lower lip as I fought off another round of giggles.

Reid shook his head. "Did you find out anything from the historical society?"

"Actually, I think I might have." I held up a finger, asking him to give me a second, and then went to find my notebook. Once I was back, I pulled my feet up under me and got comfortable before flipping to the first page of notes. "So, it's as I said, Osceola lived here and actually had a small settlement on Lake Harney. There's even an Indian burial mound, but the problem with that is that it's Timucuan and they're no longer in existence, which means there isn't a tribe to appeal to. But all of this is documented so destroying a lot of these ranches would cause a stink since they are near Lake

Harney." I tapped my notepad against one knee. "You know what I was thinking?"

"I have no clue, but you're going to tell me, right?"

I nodded. "Who decides eminent domain? Politicians. What do politicians rely on? Votes, which are heavily swayed by public opinion. You think any of them want the press that comes along with knowing that they are bulldozing history or turning Indian burial grounds into parking lots? I mean, I have more historical information for us to use, but worse case scenario, couldn't we just rely on the public justice?"

"We could, but I'd rather have an ace in my hand. My opinion is to never trust anything that you aren't personally involved with."

"Okay." I flipped through a few more pages. "We've had several different archeological teams come here because pottery pieces have been found dating back to about five hundred BC era." I kept talking even though the look on Reid's face had changed to one of amusement.

"How about wars, were any wars fought on Geneva soil?"

"The Seminole wars were fought here, and the Civil War has some history here. A lot of refugees came into Jacksonville's port and then fled down the St. John's River to seek shelter. Until eighteen twenty-one when the United States took ownership of Florida, slavery was illegal, so we were a safe harbor."

"Anything else? What about the cemetery?"

"The cemetery has seventeen documented civil war soldiers buried in it, and before you ask, no, they weren't all part of the confederate army, one was actually a union soldier. And are you ready for this?"

"Probably not." Reid winked and smiled.

"One of the buried soldiers is Lewis Powell—well, only his head is buried there, but that still counts. I guess that was all that was salvaged after he was hung for being part of the conspiracy to kill Abraham Lincoln."

"So, it's true that one of the guys was buried here, in this Podunk town?"

"Yep. Not something to put on our Welcome to Geneva sign, huh?"

"Nope, I guess not."

"I have all the dates listed of each event, names of all the soldiers, and the information about the archeology dig sites. I think we need to contact the US National Parks Services, they'll be the ones to give us more information about something being declared of historic importance."

"I'm impressed. I thought that you might find one or two things, but you have a notebook full." Reid looked more shocked than impressed, but I didn't comment. "I knew that you would do great, but this is above and beyond what I could have hoped for."

"Thanks, but it was really Miss Nancy. That woman loves to talk, even when no one is listening."

"Then I'll have to admit I'm glad you went and not me. I'm not sure I would have had the patience."

"No, you probably wouldn't have." I shifted, suddenly uncomfortable with our banter. The longer he sat across from me, the harder it was for me to keep my attention away from his lips.

"What do you think about us getting the property owners together so that we are all on the same page?"

"I say that we set it up for tomorrow night."

"At the bar?" Reid asked.

I nodded. "Friday is payday and most of the owners will be up there anyway, so it would probably be the most convenient place for a meeting."

"Perfect, what if I swing by and pick you up?"

"No need, I can meet you up there." Spending more time with him than I needed to was a bad, bad idea.

"That's crazy, we live side by side."

"I'll come over to your house and we can ride together." I needed to have some control because I felt as if I were losing every ounce in his presence.

"Fine. I'll be ready whenever you get here."

"We need to talk like this more." Reid tucked that damn strand of hair that always seemed to fall over my eyes behind my ear before heading for the door. I wanted to ask him to stay, but I couldn't seem to find the guts to say the words.

Holland walked into my stables, and for a second, I was jealous, not of another person but of my horse. He had his head hanging over his stall door and was basking in the attention that Holland was doling out to him.

"You're so gorgeous. You just look intimidating, but you're really a gentle giant, aren't you?" she crooned, and he whinnied in response, shoving his muzzle closer toward her. "Fine, fine, I'll keep loving on you. Don't you get enough attention?" Nostradamus stomped. "Don't tell me that. I've watched you and Reid, I've seen the way he treats you. He spoils you, you big fat liar." She leaned forward and placed several kisses on his long face.

I was so busy listening to her one-sided conversation that I wasn't paying attention to where I was going and ended up kicking a rake. She turned, seeing me for the first time, and I ducked my head, trying to act as if I hadn't just been eavesdropping. "Oh, you're here. I was just coming in to tell Syd goodnight before I headed up to the house to wait for you."

"Who's Syd?"

"I am." Syd's voice came from a stall a few doors down a second before he stuck his head out so she could see him.

"Holland, this is Syd. He's my stable manager." Syd was sitting on a stool conditioning the hooves on one of the racing horses that we housed for the winter.

"So, you're the one who Nostradamus was trying to impress. I heard the way he was talking to you." Holland smiled brightly, and I found I was jealous again. She had never smiled at me that way.

"He's very charming."

"He seemed like he was taken with you, you must have a way with horses. I'd love to see how Hightower responds to you."

"Who?"

Holland asked at the same time I firmly said, "No!"

She cut me a glare and then turned to Syd. "Who's Hightower?"

I shook my head, but the old fool wasn't listening to me, which made sense since, you know, I was only his boss. "He's a Thoroughbred staying with us. I have a feeling that either his owner or trainer had a heavy hand with a training whip."

"The asshole," Holland stated.

"Yep. He'll let us feed him and clean his stall, but other than that, he shies away from us. He isn't mean—"

"You don't know that." We hadn't been able to get close enough to really know if the horse was safe or not.

"He isn't. You can see it in his eyes. He's got scared eyes not evil eyes," Syd barked back at me.

"Where is he?"

"Last stall on your left," Syd said.

"We don't have time. We need to get up to the bar."

Holland ignored me, not that I was shocked.

She pulled a peppermint from her pocket—one of those Star-lite mints you grabbed by the handful as you left a restaurant—and tossed it into her mouth. When she got to Hightower's stall, she began blowing in long, slow exhales.

"What are you doing?"

She waved away my question without looking at me and continued blowing around the smell of peppermint for another minute before saying, "Peppermint is a natural calming remedy for animals. But at the same time, he's scared of people so I want to mask my human scent somewhat since peppermint is so overpowering."

"And you just happen to have them on you?"

"I always have them on me just in case I come across any strays or if one of my horses get spooked." She continued crooning to me about the peppermints as Hightower took a few tentative steps toward her, and then she held out her hand, palm up, and asked, "Can you hand me an apple or carrot?"

I moved to go get one but Syd was already there, holding one of each out to me. "Thanks," I said as I took both and passed them to Holland.

She chose the carrot, never once stopping with the whole mouth blowing. Hightower took another step forward and stretched his neck toward her. He wasn't close enough that she could actually get a grip on him, but he was close enough to reach the outstretched carrot. Once he had it, he back-stepped deeper into his stall. "What a good boy." Holland didn't move as Hightower chomped. When he was finished, she held out an apple, and this time, Hightower came a few steps closer before taking it and retreating.

"When we come back tonight, do you mind if I see him again?" Holland asked.

"No, not at all," Syd answered, and she gave him a smile that lit up her entire face. I was glad that Syd had forced the issue about Hightower because I enjoyed watching Holland interact with him.

"You ready to go?" I asked, my words sounding more clipped than I had intended. She nodded handing the bucket back over to Syd before she went to the sink near the stable doors and washed her hands.

———

The Elbow Room was crowded when we got there and we ended up having to park along the street.

"I see what you mean about everyone coming here on payday. I guess I've never been up here on a Friday night—or maybe not this early."

"Yeah, they'll all clear out before six so they can be home for supper."

I got out of the truck and hurried around, but by the time I got there, Holland was already shutting the door behind her. I shook my head.

"What?" she snapped.

"Nothing. You ready?"

"Let's go." She headed for the heavy wooden door, and I grabbed the handle before she could and pulled it open. "I know how to open a door."

"I'm sure you do. I wasn't questioning your ability. I was just being polite."

She walked in, slowing only long enough for a polite, "Thank you."

Inside the bar it didn't take long for me to realize that Holland was right, almost all of the ranchers from the community center meeting were here. Some were sitting at a table talking while others were off having a beer with who were obviously their ranch hands.

"Want to start with Mr. Brown and Mr. Kirby?" Holland tilted her head toward a table where the two sat with another man.

"Who are they with?"

"That's Everett Yarborough. His family has been part of this community since it began, they have their fingers in everything."

"I don't know him."

"Yeah, he comes in every now and then, he lives in Chuluota." Chuluota was the next town over, and it was smaller and rural like Geneva. It also had fewer ranches, but the ones it did have had more acreage.

I followed Holland as she headed over to the table and took the last empty seat, which forced me to pull a chair over from another table. "Everett, this is Reid Brooks."

I shook his hand, and we made basic introductions before he asked, "Thoroughbreds, right?"

"Yep."

"I'd love to come out and see them some time, not that I have any experience. Although, if you asked this one . . ." He stuck out an elbow and jabbed her. She smiled at him, and just like that, I hated the guy. "I shouldn't be allowed on the back of a horse again."

"Not much of a horse rider?" I asked.

"I didn't say he couldn't ride. I said he shouldn't be allowed to ride," Holland offered. "He got busted for riding while drunk when we were teenagers."

I was confused. "A cop pulled you over on your horse?"

"Welcome to small-town living. We used to have bonfires under the Snowhill bridge. Truthfully, though, I blame getting caught on Holland."

"Sure, blame me, I didn't force you to get drunk and then get on your horse, you could have walked home. I told you that I would bring her. But nooo, you had to get your ass up there and ride."

"Yeah, and I would have been fine if you"—he pointed to Holland—"hadn't held onto the reins and stood on the street screaming at the top of your lungs that you didn't care if I got killed but you weren't going to let me risk the horse's life."

Holland was laughing hysterically. "That was how the deputy found us—me holding on to the reins and screaming and Everett, who was trying to stay up but was too shit faced to sit straight."

Everett rolled his eyes. "Don't forget the best part. The deputy asks if she's Holland Kelly, she says, 'Yes, sir,' and he orders me to let her handle the horse. So, she gets on and rides off, leaving me there to deal with my own stupidity."

"What did the deputy do?" I asked.

"He called my parents because he figured I'd have a worse time of it if he handed me over to them than going to jail. Considering I got my ass beat, was grounded for the entire summer, and then got stuck doing all the shit chores, I can't imagine juvenile hall being much different."

"I'm surprised none of you kids got bitten by snakes or gators. That's murky lake water around there," Mr. Brown cut in for the first time.

"Oh, we used to do some stupid things as well when we were kids." Mr. Kirby laughed over some memory. "Anyway, what brings you two here?" I loved how he changed the subject.

"We actually came to talk with you all, I wanted to see who else was here." Holland stood and scanned the room. "Give me one second."

She moved to a table on the other side of the bar and spoke to them as she gestured toward us. Once they all started to grab their drinks and stand, I turned back to Everett.

"Has anyone told you what's been going on?" I asked him.

"They were just filling me in. I've gotta say, something doesn't sound right. The proposed properties aren't even in a straight line or connected."

"Holbrook says that's because some areas they can use are already owned by the county or have accessed roads," I explained.

"For what? Pylons? I can't imagine some of those areas being large enough to construct the infrastructure needed for this type of road or the exits and on-ramps."

I nodded. "My thoughts exactly."

"What are pylons?" Holland asked.

"They're those huge concrete support beams that the road is built on," Everett explained.

Six more men joined us and then Holland returned to her seat next to me. "Thank you for giving us a few minutes of your evening. We'll make this quick, but I'm assuming that no one sitting around this table is interested in selling their property, correct?"

All of the men nodded, some even looking downright hostile that we would have to ask.

"Good." I nodded.

"I went and spoke with Miss Nancy at the museum and she gave me an entire list of places of historic importance. I'm just waiting to hear back from the National Parks Services to see what they can help us with," Holland stated before turning to me.

"I've spoken with my attorney, and he is looking into the validity of what they are proposing. We need to figure out why he's lying to all of us about who is selling and who isn't, though. It could be a tactic just to get us all to sell, but something tells me there is more to it."

"How do you propose we do that?" Mr. Brown asked.

"Well, I've got the name of a private investigator that is supposed to be able to dig up info on anything on anyone because let's face it there's something fishy about Holbrook. A property developer bidding on a road construction project just doesn't seem to fit."

"You think he's after something else, like what?" Everett asked.

"I'm not sure exactly." The men started grumbling. "But that's what I'm hoping to find out. Until I do, I think we all need to avoid the man. And, for god's sake, whatever you do don't agree to anything or sign anything."

"What about that councilman? Is he in on it, too?" Holland asked. I sucked in my cheeks to fight back my smile, as I watched Holland bounce in her chair. She couldn't decide whether she wanted to get up and go after someone or stay here and obviously be part of the plan to ruin Johnson Holbrook.

"Just be careful, if Johnson Holbrook can hire the councilman then that means Shane Stuart is just as dirty," Mr. Brown said as he pulled out his keys from his pocket.

"Can you do us a favor?" I waited until the men nodded. "Will you get the word around to those who aren't here, let them know what we're doing? These guys aren't above lying to get people to believe them, so none of you should believe a word they say because there is no way I'm selling."

"I'm not selling either," Holland added as if the thought of doing otherwise was preposterous.

"If you all need anything, let me know," Everett added. "My dad has connections."

"Does he have any friends in Tallahassee? Particularly on the Transportation Commission?"

"Not sure, but I'll see if I can find out. If he does, do you want me to see what he can learn about this proposed expansion?"

"Please."

"Will do. If I hear anything, I'll give you a call." He looked over at Holland. "Can you text me Reid's number?"

"Sure."

Everett stood. "I'd better get out of here before Carly sends out the search party."

"Tell her I said hey," Holland offered. "Oh, and tell her to let us know what y'all still need for the baby."

"Nothing, absolutely nothing. Between my mother and hers, they've bought everything you could think to buy for a baby. I'm going to laugh if it turns out to be a girl and all of their tractors, dump trucks, and other stuff has to be sent back. It will teach them."

"That's cruel," Holland chided.

"It's the truth. Goodnight, y'all."

I stood and shook his hand, suddenly liking the man much more. I told myself that him being married and having a baby due had nothing to do with it, but who was I kidding?

"We'll talk to everyone, don't worry," Mr. Brown assured us.

"Thanks."

The men slid their chairs back and some left and others moved back to where they were before Holland had dragged them over.

I held out one hand to Holland, but she didn't take it as she stood. "Want to get a drink?"

"Sure, a beer if you don't mind." She smiled and batted her damn eyelashes.

I ordered two as we slid onto vacant stools at the bar.

"Why are you smirking?"

"I'm not." I totally was.

"Yeah, you are. You look like Sylvester right after he caught Tweetie bird."

"I don't know, maybe it has something to do with the fact that you've driven me crazy for the past two years, and then suddenly, I discover that I like having you around."

"Awww, well, don't I just feel like Old MacDonald."

"Huh?" I was totally lost but the woman's snark had me mesmerized.

"With a screw you here, and screw you there, here a screw, there a screw, everywhere a screw, screw."

"Mark my words one of these days . . ."

"One of these days, what?" Holland popped her hands on her hips.

"Nothing, oh, nothing." I waved her off. Okay, I wasn't sure what I was going to say either, I just knew that I loved aggravating the woman. While we sat there and drank, the band started, and people got up and danced. I took a swig and smiled as Holland tapped her toes, her feet softly moving with the rhythm of the song. "Want to dance?"

The song had just changed to "Everybody's Got Some-body But Me" by Hunter Hayes.

"This is a two-step, do you know how?" she asked, doubt clinging to every word.

"You'll have to find out." I held one hand out, hoping that she'd take hold, and when she did, I wanted to take a bow. Slowly but surely, I was learning how Holland Kelly operated.

With one hand around the back of her waist, I held her up against my side, as my other hand held hers in front of us. We moved in typical fashion around the dance floor—quick, quick, slow, slow.

"I can't believe that you know the two-step."

"I'm from Kentucky, which is more Southern in custom than Florida. I'm more shocked that you do."

"It's more this area, we're rednecks." Holland grinned, not meaning the term in derogatory fashion. "We like pickup trucks, cowboy boots, and country music."

As we danced, she occasionally looked over at me and smiled, which only made me want to lean down and kiss her again.

Chapter Ten

HOLLAND

Reid pulled into his garage, and I was anxious to get out and go check on Hightower. "Can I go to the stables and check on Hightower?"

"Sure. Give me a second." Reid walked over to a panel of lights and flipped a switch. Small lights that lined a brick walkway illuminated all the way to the stables.

"What else can you tell me about him?"

"Just about anything you want to know. He's three and has been in a few races. About six months ago, he stopped performing." Reid gave me tidbits of info as we walked down to the stables. "The owner sent him and another horse down to me for the winter. He's training the new one to be the racer."

"But he isn't training Hightower?"

"Nope. Our instructions were to board him and nothing else."

"Is the new horse skittish?"

"Nope, not one bit. That's why Syd and I think that someone was using a whip to try to force Hightower against his will."

"If you think Hightower was being abused, isn't there anything that you can do?"

"Nope. He isn't my horse. Animals are chattel, whether we want to admit it or not, and I can't report the owner unless I have proof."

"That's not fair." I wanted to shout at the injustice. Animals weren't chattel, a coffee table was chattel, a car was chattel, but an animal was a living thing.

When we reached the stables, I grinned at the small bucket sitting by Hightower's stall. I pulled a peppermint out and popped it into my mouth before picking up the bucket. Breathing through my mouth, I softly spoke to the horse.

"Where's my man? I came back to see you. Would you like another carrot?" I reached into the bucket and pulled a carrot out, extending it by the tip. Hightower took a few minutes to bounce around his small confinement, lifting his front hooves off the ground and snuffling a bunch of times before he settled.

"Well, someone's excited to see me." He slowly inched over and took the carrot. This time, he didn't retreat, though. "What a brave man, I promise I won't hurt you, you can trust me." I slowly slid my hand back. I didn't want to give him anymore snacks for fear he'd associate me with only food. So, I stood there talking softly, Hightower's big expressive eyes locked with mine. Occasionally, I would glance over to Reid, who had a strange look on his face. He wasn't smiling, but he wasn't frowning either.

After about thirty minutes, I decided that it was time to go. Hightower wasn't moving any closer, so I would try again tomorrow if it was okay with Reid.

"Why don't you come back to the house, we can have a drink and then I'll drive you over to your house?"

"No need to drive, I can cut across the lawn."

"Then I'll walk you over to your apartment afterward."

I nodded and followed Reid around the stables as he locked up and then back up to his house. "Want a beer, wine, or something else?"

"Wine or beer is fine."

"I'll grab it, why don't you have a seat."

I moved into the sunroom and went to move a sketchpad out of my way so I could sit. Curiosity got the better of me, and before I set the book aside, I opened it to a random page.

I stared at it—the long braided hair and the detailed fleurde-lis pattern on the boots that resembled the pair I owned. The same boots I was wearing tonight. Flipping through the pages, I realized that they were all of me. In almost all of them, I was riding Khan, but some were of me simply sitting underneath a tree or walking to the stables.

I looked up when Reid cleared his throat. "Did you draw these?" He set the wine glasses down and reached to snag the sketchpad from me, but I moved it away from him. "No. Tell me, did you draw these?"

"Yes."

"When? How?"

"I find it relaxing." He had turned to look out the back wall of windows.

"That doesn't answer my questions."

"I see you out riding mornings, and that's when I'm in here drawing."

"But what about the other drawings when I'm not riding?"

"Happenstance, I guess. I usually just draw what I see."

"So, it could have been anything or anyone?" I asked.

"Yes."

I flipped through the pad again, totally wanting to call bullshit but I could tell that he was uncomfortable, and for once, I didn't want to give him a hard time. "They're beautiful, but you really should focus on something that can show your talent better." I gave him a wicked smile as I reached for the wine he'd brought me. Yes, I was totally fishing for compliments.

Reid let out a sigh of relief and moved to take a seat next to me. "I'll take that into consideration. All I had chilled was Riesling, it's what Ellie likes."

"Is she going to be mad?"

"No, she has several bottles in there, but if she is, I'll buy her more."

We sat in silence, staring out at the night sky and enjoying the wine. "Do you do anything else besides sketch? Have any other hidden talents?"

Reid raised one eyebrow, and I felt my cheeks grow warm because he was clearly reading more into that question than I meant. "Nope, just drawing. How about you? Any special talents?"

"I can tie a cherry stem with my tongue." Okay, that was lame, but there wasn't much that was remarkable about the youngest Kelly sibling.

"That's some mad tongue skills."

"You have no idea."

His attention drops to my lips, and I stood far too abruptly to avoid looking like a scared bunny and took two steps toward the door. "Thanks for the wine." I turned, and he was right behind me. God, I wanted to kiss him, so . . . I did.

I brushed my fingertips over his cheek and tried not to get hypnotized by the sensation. Our eyes met, and the arousal I'd been denying this past week warmed me. There was something totally different from anything I'd seen before looking back at me from his dark blue eyes. It was still the same determination I'd seen as we planned our strategy but this time his eyelids were heavy, and his jaw was tensed, it sent heat between my legs, and I could hear myself panting.

My voice was all whispery when I said, "Thanks for tonight, I probably should head home."

He drifted closer. "I think that you should probably stay." His voice was raspy like he, too, was fighting for control. Reid's eyelids dropped, and his dark lashes brushed against his cheekbones. "God, Holland, I want you so fucking bad." He wrapped one arm around me and pulled me flush against his body. I could feel just how badly he wanted me. He lowered his mouth to mine and kissed me slowly, as if he wasn't in a hurry to devour every inch of me.

His hands slid to my hips, and he lifted me before pressing me back against the wall and urging my legs to wrap around him.

Holding tight, he moved a hand and gripped the back of my neck as he leaned in and kissed me. The only sound in the room were our breaths mixing like music, a song that I couldn't seem to get enough of. I was holding onto his shoulders, and god, the man was solid. Tugging at his shirt, I forced myself to pull it up slowly when what I really wanted to do was rip it from his body. His mouth assaulted my neck. Holy hell, I forgot what I was doing as his tongue slid to my earlobe and sparks danced over my skin as his teeth nipped. I needed air—no, that wasn't it, I needed release.

"Oh my god, Holland, I need to be inside you."

"Take me to your secret lair." I smiled and winked.

"Makes me sound like a monster," he groaned as he slid a hand under my shirt and cupped my breast.

"Or a beast."

"I'll show you a beast."

"Brag much?" But I had already felt him, I knew that he wasn't bragging, but I couldn't stop myself from aggravating him.

He turned and carried me, I hadn't really had a chance to look at his home, and part of me wanted to do that but at the same time, I wanted him. I found the best of both worlds kissing his collarbone. Don't judge, I know that I looked like a friggin' vampire, but I could kiss and look over his shoulder as he carried me up the sprawling staircase. It was like something out of *Gone With the Wind*. I kissed as he passed several closed doors and then moved into what I figured was his bedroom. If it wasn't his, someone was in for a shock.

His king-size bed was situated under a large half-moon shaped window, and he came to a stop next to it. He slowly let my legs down and held me close to him until he was sure that I was steady on my feet.

"Get up on the bed," he ordered. I kicked off my shoes and then crawled onto the thick comforter. "Stand up."

I did as ordered and then turned to face him. Apparently, I wasn't close enough because he pulled me forward so that I was right in front of him and he was level with my pussy. "Hold on, sweetheart, I'll be with you in a second." He leaned forward and blew hot air that seemed to soak through the denim and make me very aware of just how soaked my panties were.

With one hand, he pulled the button on my jeans free and then tugged the zipper down. Then he slowly slid them down my legs and helped me step out of them.

For a moment I freaked, totally forgetting which panties I had worn, but a glance told me I was in my Friday ones. For once, I was wearing the right panties on the right day. I usually just reached in and grabbed a pair. As long as they were clean, what did I care?

Slowly he came around and cupped my butt, his fingertips softly massaging my cheeks.

"Are you sure?" His voice slipped into a husky timbre.

Actions were louder than words so I dropped to my knees and kissed him. He kissed me back, and my tongue slipped inside and tangled with his. That was all the control he let me have before he was pressing forward and demanding more from me. A small whimper slid from my mouth. I couldn't think, and I could hardly breathe while I was experiencing one of the most soul-stealing kisses of my life.

The feel of him so close, the warmth of his skin, his tongue continuing to plunge deeper each time it found mine. The air between us sparked, and he caught my bottom lip between his teeth and bit it softly.

His hands trailed down my sides, curving over my hips and then hooking under me to bring my legs out so that I was flat on my back and my legs were hanging off the bed. He slowly slid my panties down as he let out a chuckle.

"What's so funny?"

"You. Do you normally forget the day of the week and need to check your underwear to be certain?"

"Shut up and get undressed."

He was grinning as he pulled back, and I propped myself up on my elbows, ready for the show. I didn't dare blink for fear that I might miss something as he toed off his boots and then pulled his T-shirt over his head. Holy hell, he was built. Okay, I knew the man was in shape, but this should be illegal. He even had that perfectly formed V that slightly showed above the waistband of his jeans, and I was dying to get my hands on it.

When he unbuttoned the top button of his Levi button-fly jeans, I held my breath. Was he a boxer or briefs guy or maybe a boxer brief guy? Please, just no tighty whities.

When the last button was undone and he slid his jeans off I felt like I should do penitence because the man was commando and his cock . . . oh my lord, it was huge.

He opened his nightstand and pulled out a condom packet, which had shivers racing down my spine and goose pimples tingling over my skin. He laid it on the bed next to my hip and then settled one knee between my legs.

"Yes, Reid." I bucked, pushing my hips up to deepen his touch. Everything—his touch, his smell, his passion—was overwhelming, and it was all for me. Every muscle in my stomach contracted in time with his fingers as they slid in and out of me.

His mouth switched breasts and then lifted so that he was kissing my lips harder than before. His mouth slipped below my left ear and started nibbling and sucking.

"God, Reid, please."

"Please what?"

"I don't know. Just god."

My neck was the most sensitive part of my body, and the evening stubble that peppered his jawline was sending a wildfire to my brain. He chuckled against my skin and nipped playfully along my jaw.

Each kiss had me getting wetter.

I wrapped my hand around his cock and stroked him a few times, but then he was hooking an arm under my knee and lifting my leg so that I was open to him. His strong fingertips softly stroked my clit before sinking a finger deep inside me. My legs jerked and held on to him tighter as nerves sang through my body. His mouth dropped back to my breast while his fingers continued their assault. At first just one and then two, over and over and *over* again. The sensations were too much.

"R-Reid—" I gasped, feeling my body starting to lock up. "I'm going to come."

He didn't stop but sped up, driving my body higher until I exploded.

My body was still quaking and his fingers were still stroking in and out of me slowly as my hand slipped between us. His gasp of breath as I wrapped my fingers around his cock was an aphrodisiac. He had so much heat trapped in his dick and my mind was whirling with all the ways I could help him release it.

His cheek rubbed against mine as his teeth nibbled at my ear.

"Fuck, Holland," he groaned as I slid my hand up and down his cock. "I want you."

Before I could say a word, he was over me. His hands squeezing my hips, holding me down as if he thought I were going to go somewhere. Not on his life.

His fingers shook as he ripped the foil and pulled out the latex to sheath his cock. Holding my breath, I waited until he was between my legs and then I guided his cock to my entrance.

He sank into me in one fluid motion. "Oh, fuckkk." His words were a cross between a moan and a groan.

My back arched and my mouth let out a guttural gasp as he stilled deep within me.

"Jesus, Holland," Reid hissed, his muscles straining as he held himself back until I adjusted to him.

Reid moved slowly at first before picking up his pace, and I pushed up to meet each thrust as he pounded into me. Grabbing my leg, he lifted it and stretched me so that it was over my head and he was deep, deeper than I'd ever imagined. His rhythm was hard but so fucking perfect. Tilting my hips, I tried to meet his thrusts, but the need inside me was begging for release and it was all I could do to hold it back because I didn't want this one to end.

Reid apparently wasn't willing to let me keep what bit of control I was clinging to because his thrusts turned to slow and deep as he rocked against me so he was rubbing against my clit with a delicious pressure.

"Fuckkkkk—"

I reached up and pulled our mouths together as my vision blurred under the onslaught of pleasure.

"God, you're so fucking beautiful." He didn't stop as my body gripped him and my heart tried to hammer its way out of my chest. The more he moved inside me, the longer my orgasm stretched until I was ready to beg him to stop.

Then, like a flick of a switch, his thrusts turned to pounding once again, I could feel his cock hardening. My hands slipped along his sweat-slicked shoulders and I wrapped my legs around his waist pulling him into me. My body quivered as his cock pulsed inside me. My name mingled with the word fuck as his muscles stiffened and his eyelids squeezed closed.

Exhausted, he collapsed and I prepared myself to hold his weight but he caught himself on his forearms and stayed raised. Locking eyes his jaw twisted, and he kissed me on my cheek before moving to my mouth. Only then did I unwind my legs from him and allow him to pull out.

Chapter Eleven

REID

I slid one arm out to pull Holland back against me, but all I felt were sheets—cool, empty sheets.

"Fuck." After jumping from bed, I moved to pull on my jeans and grabbed a shirt. Then I hobbled and hopped as I tried to slip my shoes on as I made my way downstairs to see if she was still here. I knew better, though. Holland was long gone.

"Morning, don't you look like death ran over?" Ellie greeted me when I came around the corner into the kitchen. "Must have been a wild night."

I raised a brow, wondering how she knew. "Did you see her?"

"Who? Your fuck buddy? Nope." She grinned as I glared. Holland was not a fuck buddy. I bit my tongue as I turned to the window and looked toward the Kelly stables, but the doors weren't open yet.

"What's up with you?"

"Nothing."

"Something is, you aren't acting normal."

"Okay, let me rephrase that. There is nothing wrong that I want to talk to my baby sister about."

"Wow, you sure are surly for someone who got laid last night. Oh, wait, did she leave before putting out? You poor thing. Let me fix you some coffee and then you can go take a nice cold shower." Ellie grabbed my mug and filled it for me.

"Remind me again, when are you getting your own place to live?"

"No clue. You said that your house was big enough since it was just you. Anyway, here you go." She handed me my mug. "I have to get going, today's my early day so I have to be at my first appointment by six thirty."

I shook my head. "A bit early for dog grooming, isn't it?"

"They want me to have it done before they leave for work. I only do this once a week. Most of my clients give me a key or garage code access." Ellie picked up her lunchbox and headed out to her mobile pet grooming van.

I knew it was early, but Holland was always up before the sun, so I snagged my phone and dialed her. For some reason, I wasn't surprised when the call went to voice mail.

"This is Holland Kelly, if you are calling and were not personally given my number by me then you are a solicitor. I charge all solicitors twenty-five dollars per call. This message serves as notice, and all future calls from you will be billed to you and or your company."

I laughed because it was epic Holland. When the tone finally buzzed, I spoke. "Call me, I didn't like not finding you next to me this morning when I woke up." I ended the call and then made my way to my office and got some bills paid and then I headed down to the stables.

"Good morning, Syd."

Syd looked up from Slipper's stall. "Morning?" He glanced at his watch. "It's almost afternoon."

"Ha ha, very funny. It isn't even nine."

"Considering I'm used to seeing you around six, I'd say that is afternoon. You just missed Holland."

"She was here?"

"Yep, she came over to spend a few minutes with High-tower. I thought maybe she was heading up to the house since she asked if I'd seen you yet this morning."

"I must have missed her. I'll go see what she needed." It took every ounce of self-restraint I had not to run out of the stables to find her. I had zero hopes that Syd was fooled, though.

The hellion was mucking out a stall. "Asking about me this morning, huh?" I smiled when she jumped, happy to catch her off guard.

"No. I went over to see Hightower."

"Hmmm. Why did you sneak out this morning?" Holland looked around before answering.

"I didn't sneak out. I got up and left. You were sound asleep, and I didn't want to wake you."

That seemed reasonable enough, but the irrational side of me still didn't like it. "Would you like to come over tonight? I'll cook."

"No."

"No? Just no?" I shoved my hands into my pockets. It was the only thing that was going to keep me from wringing her pretty neck.

"Reid, last night was a mistake. We don't even like each other." She kicked at some hay that had fallen. "We got carried away. We're stressed by everything with Holbrook, and we found a common ground in fighting this development deal. But when this is all over, we will go back to being two people who never speak."

"We used to talk."

"No, we used to make digs at each other. Me, giving you the bird doesn't count as talking. Neither does me cussing you out. You and I would never work; we're just too different."

"Well, yes we are, I'm glad you figured that out. I thought they would have taught you the difference back in . . . I don't know, sixth grade? Boys have this thing called a—" Holland threw a hand over my mouth.

"Shut up. That isn't what I meant."

"Fine, then what did you mean?"

"How many acres is your property?" Holland tapped the toe of her boot as she waited for me to answer.

"Five hundred more or less."

"That is a hundred acres more than we have, and you don't even have cattle."

"So, I don't see your point."

"How far did you go in school?"

"All the way." Holland raised one eyebrow and waited. My answer obviously hadn't been enough. "I have my bachelors."

"I graduated high school. Your stable houses how many horses?"

"I don't see what this has to do with anything."

"Just answer the question, Reid."

"Forty-eight."

"Iron Horse houses ten."

"So?"

"So? So?" Holland threw her hands up. "Open your eyes, you and me, we come from two totally different worlds. We aren't poor, but we aren't Thoroughbreds. You are a Thoroughbred, Triple crown, Belmont, Preakness . . . you get the idea. I'm not like you, and I'm okay with that. I like who I am."

"I like who you are, too . . . most days. Well, the days you aren't throwing crap at my house."

Holland let out a resounding sigh. "Let's just concentrate on Holbrook, last night can't happen again. Okay?"

Yeah, I wasn't okay with that. So, I leaned in to give her a kiss before she had a second to pull back. "The way your body trembled when I was inside you wasn't a mistake."

Before she could deny it, I turned and left.

By the time I got back to my house, it was close to noon, I headed to my office to get it over with and call Brandy.

"Hello?"

Her voice sounded exactly the same.

"Hey, Brandy. It's Reid Brooks."

"Wow, Reid. Long time, huh?"

"Yep. It's been what? Fourteen years." We were both quiet for a few seconds.

"Something like that, how have you been?"

"Great. I'm down in Florida now, running my own stables."

"Lucky you." She laughed, and I totally understood. If she were still in Kentucky, she would be dealing with the thick of winter. "Your brother said your parents were pissed when you left, but I say good for you. You were always meant to do more than work for your brother."

"Thanks." I cleared my throat. "Listen, I hope you don't mind, but I got your number from Adler. He said you helped him out with some problems he was having a few years back, and I was wondering if you could help me with something."

"What kind of issues are you having?" Brandy's voice had taken on a pure business-like demeanor.

I started at the beginning and ended when I walked into the Elbow Room and busted Holbrook for lying to everyone about how I'd signed the paperwork.

"Okay," she said. "I agree that there is something strange about the councilman being involved, and there are legal repercussions for coercing people to sign contracts, but we would have to have proof."

"I'm sure we can get proof if we need it, but I don't think

anyone has actually signed anything yet. What else do you need from me to get started?"

"I'm going to need the addresses of as many of the properties that he's trying to acquire, as well as the contact information for the owners. If you can forward me any of the letters you've received from Johnson Holbrook, his attorney, the county, or the state, that would also be helpful. My email address is checkmate at brandylakote dot com." I smiled at the address. Hopefully, she could help us checkmate Holbrook. "Send me what you have, and I'll send you a contract."

"Sounds good."

"Okay. Then, I'll catch a flight down to Jacksonville to see if I can dig up anything on road expansion plans for your area before heading your way."

"Thank you. You really have no idea how much I appreciate you being willing to help."

"No problem. If there's anything crooked, I'll find it, I promise." Brandy disconnected, and I got to work scanning the documents she'd requested.

I spent the rest of the day gathering info for Brandy, only stopping to sign and return the contract. That and to recover from the mini heart attack I had when I saw the fee she charged. But, then again, I wasn't doing this for just me. I was doing it for Holland and everyone else in this town.

———

It had been two days since . . . well . . . since our night, and I wanted to talk with her. I hadn't had the chance to tell her about Brandy, who was arriving sometime today. I tried calling her, no answer. I tried catching her when she came over to see Hightower, but the girl had an uncanny sense of knowing when I wouldn't or couldn't be there.

I grabbed my cup of coffee and I headed outside to wait for her to come back from her ride with Khan. But before I had a chance to drink the whole cup, she rounded the bend and I waved at her to stop.

"Whoa."

"What do you want, Reid?" She pulled back on Khan's reins and gave me an annoyed look.

"I'm not sure why you're avoiding me."

"I'm not avoiding you. I've just been super busy. You have Syd and those other guys, but I only have myself. So, that means that I have to work. Sorry."

"Bullshit. You and I both know that this has nothing to do with you being busy."

"No? Okay, how about this? I don't feel comfortable around you."

"Umm, darling, you were quite comfortable having you around me the other night."

"Stop, will you? What makes you think that saying something like to me or anyone would be okay? So, what? Because we slept together once that means you have some claim on me and can just say whatever you want like you have some right? Have you lost your mind?"

"You know that wasn't how I meant it. Damn it, Holland." I raked my hand through my hair and blew out a deep breath. "One of these days, you're going to have to grow up. You may be the youngest of your family, but you're an adult, and it's time to start acting like it. Running away when things get hard, scary, or complicated is bullshit. Throwing shit on someone's house because you have half a story is immature. Avoiding phone calls and throwing around accusations like you just did is—" I stopped and raked a hand through my hair. "You know what? Never mind. I just came out here to tell you that the investigator called, and she has information for us about Holbrook."

"She?"

"Yes, she. She'll be here around four, and I'd like it if you were at the meeting so you can hear what she has to say, too."

Holland shook her head. "Okay, but if I come over, it's just for business, got it?"

I stared at her dumbfounded. I had no clue why she was looking at me as if I were to blame for everything.

"It's just that . . . what happened between us . . . it can't happen again. We don't like each other."

"Yeah. Got it. You don't like me and have no interest in sleeping with me." How she managed to sell that lie to herself was beyond me, but sometimes you had to pick and choose your battles. This was not a battle I wanted to fight right then and there. "Just come over so you can meet her and hear everything for yourself."

Pissed off, I turned and headed to work off some of my anger in the stables. When the sound of Khan's hooves could be heard thundering in the opposite direction, I didn't look back.

I wasn't sure how long I had sat in the corner with sheep cloth and a bottle of Neatsfoot oil and conditioned the tack since it hadn't been done in a few months. As I scrubbed, I worked through Holland's words. She was scared of what? Me? No, that couldn't be it. Was it that she was afraid to be vulnerable? I wasn't sure whether I was giving my muscles more of a workout or my brain. Finally I gave up the ghost and put everything away then headed up to the house.

When I got inside, I grabbed my phone and read the text waiting for me.

Brandy Lakote: I'm at the Seminole County courthouse, pulling records on your property and the other two you sent me. Did you know that there hasn't been an actual land survey completed in years on any property except yours and that was only done because you ordered it before you purchased?

Me: No, is this important?

Brandy Lakote: There would have to be one so they knew the land was stable for road construction and to determine fair-market value. Eminent domain is still technically a sale so they have to be done prior to making offers.

Me: Does this mean Holbrook is making the whole thing up?

Brandy Lakote: All three of the properties you gave me info on have had a Survey of Sustainable Management completed within the last three months. I'm going to try to contact the geophysicist who signed these surveys and then I will be out to your house.

Me: Thanks.

I traded my phone for my laptop and spent the next hour reading about what a geophysicist did as well as sustainable management surveys.

Chapter Twelve

HOLLAND

Damn it. I hated the way he made me feel. Why did he have to be so damn good looking? Couldn't he be at least . . . I don't know . . . ugly? God, those eyes—they were the color of the deepest part of the ocean and so blue that, at times, they appeared black. I knew that I was what made him as unsteady as a storm thundering one minute and lightning and hailing the next. But damn it all to hell, he did the same thing to me. My insides were a knotted mess, and I was so fucking confused.

I held out my hands in front of me and examined my nails. I've never had a manicure. Hell, what woman my age has never had a manicure? And truth be told, I didn't care if I ever had one. Could you imagine someone like me at the Kentucky Derby? First person to see my hands would be asking me to bring them a Brown Betty. Wait, was that a drink or a dessert? Shit, never mind.

My feet were propped up on the coffee table and I was staring at the giant stone fireplace where my sisters and I spent way too many nights roasting marshmallows and pretending we were having a campfire.

"You're awful quiet today," London said, taking the seat to my right.

"Just a lot on my mind."

"Like what?"

"Do I act like a kid?"

London looked over her shoulder toward Paris as she came into the living room and plopped down on the sofa on the other side of me.

"I have to say that you've grown more in the last few months than you had in the last few years. But part of it is our fault." London waved to herself and Paris.

"How is it your fault?"

"You were almost four when mom left, Paris was seven, I was ten. I think that we tried to raise you. Instead of having one mom, you got two plus Daddy. I think that we probably protected you more than we should have and never pushed you to grow up because of our own guilt. Dad saw how much you loved horses and wanted to nurture that to get you away from us."

Paris giggled. "I think he was getting tired of us doing things for you. We would constantly tell him stuff like that you wanted like chocolate chip cookies so I had to make them."

"But I hate chocolate chip cookies."

Paris giggled again. "I know, but London and I loved them and knew that he couldn't say no to you."

"Awww, okay."

"I think Dad finally figured it out and started to worry that we weren't allowing you to be your own person, so when he saw your love for horses and knew that neither of us were horse crazy, he encouraged you. Even after that, though, you only had to handle your horse."

"But I'm twenty-six, that doesn't explain why I'm still like this, does it?"

Paris reached over and dragged her fingers through my hair, which always used to soothe me.

"No, it doesn't, but old habits are hard to break. What prompted all of this anyway?"

I debated whether I should say something, and then realized that there was zero point in trying to hide it. So, I dropped my face into my open palms and mumbled, "I slept with Reid."

London and Paris each reached over and pulled one hand away from my face. When I glanced at them, they were both laughing. "Care to repeat that without your hands? It was sort of garbled." London asked.

"Yeah, cause it sort of sounded like you slept with someone named Weed." Paris paused. "Holy shit, Reid. You slept with Reid."

I pulled my hands from their grasps and buried my face again, but there wasn't anything I could do to shut out the noise of them jumping around and dancing. "Will you both stop? My god, you are married women."

They weren't listening to me.

"I can't wait to call Braden and tell him that he owes me twenty bucks," London said between fits of giggles.

"Oh my god, does Ellie know?" Paris asked me.

I shrugged, having no clue whether Reid would tell his sister something like that. "Will you both sit? I'm serious."

"Hi, serious, I'm London, and you just made me twenty dollars richer."

"Ha ha." I stood and flipped them both off.

"Holland, stop. We're just kidding. We're so happy for you. We've both thought that you and him would be perfect together," London said as she wrapped one arm around my shoulders and tried to tug me back down to the couch. "We always just assumed you were mean to him as a way of flirting."

What the hell?

Paris nodded. "You know how boys are mean to little girls they like, pulling their braids and stuff like that? We thought that was what you were doing."

"No. The man seriously gets on my nerves. That one night was a mistake. That was all, it won't happen again. Sure, he's good looking, but I couldn't care less if he went and slept with another woman. I'm not interested." I had a strange ache around my heart. It was heartburn, that was all—or so I told myself.

"Why are you so opposed to giving him a chance?" Paris's soft voice seemed to break through my thoughts.

"I'm not opposed to anything, the truth is that I'm a realist."

"Real? No, the word is *realize*, as in, when are you going to realize that we are all different? London sees a glass as half-empty, I see things more as half-full, but you? You immediately think someone is out to break your glass. You need to stop, not everything is a battle, so stop looking for opponents."

"I think Paris said everything I wanted to say." London reached forward and took hold of one of my hands. "It's okay to be scared." I reluctantly agreed with them—if only to myself—I wasn't scared, not truthfully. I was just looking at the big picture, our two different worlds. God, who was I kidding, there was so much to figure out. Holbrook first and then Reid.

"Now that we've covered this, can we talk about you feeling grown-up?" I nodded at London's question. "You have your own home, you pay your bills, and have the stables, which earn enough income to keep it running. I don't know about you, but that kind of seems like you tick all the right boxes for being an adult."

"Okay, so why can't I seem to act like one?"

Paris leaned over toward me and let out a long sigh. "Holland, Holland, Holland. Let's see, calling someone Dick instead of their first name, locking the door just as they are getting ready to walk in, flipping them off whenever you see them? Is it mature? Maybe not, but it's you. And I don't ever want you to change. I love it."

"Me, too. I always know that you will make me laugh. Of the three of us you've always had the more fun side," London agreed.

"How about throwing shit on their house?"

"What?" Paris and London bellowed in unison.

"Ummm, remember the other day when you told me to stay calm? Well, I didn't. It wasn't like I planned on doing it. It kind of happened."

"I have no clue how someone just happens to get manure on another person's home, but yeah that one was pretty childish. Let me ask you this, though. What did you do after?"

I held my hands up in surrender. "I went back and cleaned it all off."

"Before or after he saw it?" Paris asked.

"After."

"Was this before or after you slept with him?" Paris asked.

"Good point," London added.

"Umm, before, why?"

"Well, at least we know he isn't holding any grudges. If he was, then you probably worked them out of him." London and Paris laughed . . . at my expense.

"Ha ha, fuck you both."

"Seriously, Holland, you need to stop acting like this and evaluate your feelings for him. Not what you think he might feel or what you think may happen—what you truly feel for him. If not, one day you're going to wake up and realize that he's moved on." Paris nodded her agreement.

I leaned my head against back of the couch and looked at the ceiling. God, why was this so hard?

"Did we help at all?" Paris wrapped one arm around me.

I pinched my index and thumb together and then separated them just a tiny bit. "A little . . ." Then I threw my arms around them and pulled them in for a giant group hug. "Okay, gotta get stuff done." I jumped up and headed for the door.

"Holland." Paris stopped me before I opened it. "So, how good was the sex?"

London busted out laughing.

I flipped them both off before hightailing it back for the stables.

Chapter Thirteen

REID

I answered my door and smiled. I wasn't sure how I would feel seeing Brandy after so many years, but as she smiled back, my nerves settled. Her hair was just as coal black, and if it weren't for the tiny lines at the corners of her eyes, I would have thought she was still eighteen. She was still just as breathtaking, and I felt absolutely nothing.

Her demeanor was much colder than Holland's, with her shoulders pulled back, and head held high. Plus, her outfit was way too . . . I didn't know . . . big city? Sure, she looked nice, but I loved the blue jeans and boots look of Holland much more.

"Reid, you haven't changed one bit." Brandy held out one hand for me to shake. It was so formal it was awkward.

"I was thinking the exact same thing about you." I cast a glance over Brandy's shoulders to try to see if Holland was approaching, but she was nowhere in sight.

Brandy followed my glance. "Are we waiting for someone?"

"Yeah, my neighbor was supposed to join us, but maybe she got held up."

"Oh, is that the Kelly Ranch?"

"Yes, there are three girls that run it." I took one step back to move out of the open doorway. "Well, come on in, she can join in when she gets here."

Brandy followed me inside. "Your house is lovely. I noticed that you named your ranch the same as your family ranch back home. What exactly is it that you do here? Is it different from back home?"

"Very different. I'm a winter boarding facility and a rehabilitation center. I'm not involved in the race circuit, but a number of the horses are racehorses. If someone tells me that they are going to start their horse in claim races, then I'll work on improving speed while the horse is with me, but that is as far as my involvement goes."

"You seem happy, you must like what you're doing."

"I do. I still get to work with Thoroughbreds, which I love, but this is separate from my family's business, so I have the freedom to run it my own way. What about you, how did you get into private investigator services?" I asked as we moved to the kitchen.

"In college, I thought that I wanted to be a lawyer, but then I wanted to be a police woman, so I switched to criminal justice. In one of the classes, an investigator who spoke with us used to be an expert computer hacker and had competed in the Cyberlympics."

"The what?"

"It is an international challenge, where computer hackers gather and try to hack into systems. There are challenges where they are given time limits and criteria where they have to circumvent certain systems. Companies and government agencies actually pay big bucks to have their systems up to be tried. Can you imagine knowing you have the top hacker on your team? Great boon for the CIA."

"Wow, I never even fathomed this."

"I know, right. Needless to say, I was entranced, I had always loved computers, but she showed me how to use these skills to help the regular person like you and me. She and I instantly bonded. She took me under her wing and well as they say . . ."

"The rest is history," we both said in unison.

"Did you stay in Texas after college?"

"Actually no, I only stayed down there for two years, it was way too hot for me, I transferred to Northwestern and that is where I still live. I love Chicago. I find that a more central location makes it easier to get wherever I need to be." Brandy set a briefcase on the table and pulled out several sets of scientific data sheets. "Well, let's get started." She pointed to the top page. "These are the sustainable surveys I had mentioned. Actually, they are magnetometry surveys, they test the ground for phosphates."

"Is that what he's after? He thinks our land has phosphates? Most of the phosphate mines have been found almost two hours away."

"That's my best guess based on the three properties you sent me. I won't know until I can look into the other properties, though."

I got up and grabbed a folder off the counter. "Here you go."

"Perfect. Now, what can you tell me about the Kelly Ranch? Holbrook has had several different surveys done on that property. It seems like he is almost fixated on it."

I nodded. "I'm not sure I can tell you much. It's just over four hundred acres, and I'm pretty sure their father owned it before they were born. You would have to ask them for specifics." I stared at the documents, trying to make sense of the numbers. "How are these tests done? I mean, wouldn't they have to be on the property to do them?"

"Yes, they would need access. Depending on whether it

was purely surface magnetic or they had to actually drill down matrix samples."

"How would they do that?"

Brandy grabbed a notebook and flipped until she found the page she was looking for. "They would use a wide-bit type auger to drill a hole, similar to how a well would be dug but just not as deep. Water is added to form a thick slurry. This is how they grade the phosphate and remove the pebbles."

"Are there any of those types of reports or surveys in the files?"

"No, but I spoke to the geophysicist that did these studies, and he said he completed a slurry test to test the minerals around the same time. He couldn't confirm which property they came from, though."

"So, you're telling me that Holbrook is illegally trespassing on our property and testing our land without our permission?"

"I'm telling you that someone is."

"Did this geophysicist tell you who hired him?"

"Yes. Maverick Trust, I have a call into them. The number is a cell phone and not showing up in any databases."

"Anything else? Did you find out anything about Councilman Stuart?"

She flipped through a dozen papers before looking up at me. "Do you know his wife?" I shook my head. "Valerie Holbrook."

"Holbrook, as in—"

"Johnson Holbrook's daughter, yep. Shane is his son-in-law."

"Why isn't this disclosed anywhere?"

"They were married before he ran for office, and Valerie prefers to stay out of the media."

I dragged one hand down my face, not believing what I

was hearing. "So, he's just supporting whatever Holbrook is after?"

"That's how it looks, but I'm still digging."

"Okay. Did you find anything on the road expansion?"

"Nope. I went through the minutes from the state and county legislative meetings and couldn't find anything. Speaking of which, tell Arthur I appreciate all his help. He walked me through all of the eminent domain procedures since they differ from state to state, and then he filled me in on all of the exceptions such as historical, public use, and hardship reasons. I was actually feeling the time crunch trying to go through all the statutes and then compare it to the surveys."

"I'm happy the two of you were able to get somewhere."

"I do have a call in to speak with someone from the Transportation Commission, I'll let you know as soon as I hear something." Brandy started folding the graphs and surveys and slipping them back into her briefcase. "Here's my business card, all of my contact numbers are on there. If anything should happen, say you hear from Holbrook, his attorney, or if he shows up here, please let me know immediately." She paused for several seconds. "You look good, Reid. I mean that."

"So do you. Seems that life is going great for you."

"You, too."

Brandy stood and headed for my front door. When we got to the bottom of the steps, she turned. "Oh, one final question."

"Yes?"

"How far am I going?" I gave her a quizzical look totally confused by her question. "What I mean is, am I looking for enough information to use to force him to leave you all alone or am I gathering enough to ruin the man and probably put him behind bars?"

"I want him to leave everyone alone, but if you happen to come across something that will do him in, then please let me know."

"You haven't changed one bit."

"Why is that?"

"Ruining him is not your main focus, living in peace is."

"Is that weird?"

"Actually, yes. People can get very vindictive." Brandy smiled and then stepped closer to give me a quick hug. "Take care, I'll be in touch soon." When she stepped back, her eyes were glistening with moisture. "This is going to sound crazy, but seeing you makes me feel old. It seems like a lifetime ago that we were in high school."

I shoved my hands into my jeans pockets. "It was a life-time ago, but I wouldn't change it for the world. We had a good time."

"We did, didn't we?"

I nodded, and with one last smile, Brandy walked off, got in her rental car, and drove away.

Chapter Fourteen

HOLLAND

Once I got to the stables, I thought about Reid asking me to join him to talk with the private investigator. I knew he said this was the person his brother had used and that she did a great job, and I refused to believe that it bothered me because I was jealous.

I do not care whether he hired a man, woman, or mule, I'm not going.

Lie. Lie. Lie.

I did care. I cared because, for some reason, the thought of walking in there and watching that woman hit on him was nauseating.

Trying to take my mind off the clock, I brushed out Khan's mane. My eyes constantly watching the minute hand as it moved, five minutes after four, ten minutes, fifteen, when it was finally forty minutes, I figured I had proven my point. I could go over, still get filled in on what the investigator had to say, and then leave. Right? Yeah, that was the plan.

I rode Khan over to Reid's, and when his front door came into view, I saw him standing there talking to the investigator.

I pulled Khan to a stop and watched as she moved to hug him. That was not how you said goodbye to someone you didn't know. The smile he gave her when she released him was one of familiarity.

It ate at me.

She was everything I wasn't. She had long, raven-black hair where mine was dirty blonde. She wore fuck-me heels and I was wearing muddy boots. Everything inside me was turning upside down as I came to the realization that I had feelings for Reid. My heart pounding, my lungs tightened making it almost impossible to breathe, like the reins had somehow wrapped around me and they were cutting off my air supply. I knew that wasn't the case because I held them in my hands. That was when I realized I was standing right out in the open and that if Reid were to look to his left, he would see me. Turning Khan around, I kicked my heels in and urged him to take off.

Damn it, I never have luck.

"Holland!" Reid hollered, but I ignored him.

I raced back toward my property, and if Khan were younger, I'd jump the fence like we used to. He wasn't, so I had to go through the front gates and down the drive. Then I was racing across the pasture at break neck speed. We had right at four hundred acres, so by the time I got to the far perimeter fence that edged the road, I was as far away as possible from one Mr. Dick Brooks, and that was exactly where I wanted to be.

Following the line, Khan cut around a few cattle that were too lazy to budge at the sound of a galloping horse. When I got to the end, I cut left and followed the back line of our property that butted up to the woods. Khan finally slowed when we were approaching the last turn, and I clutched the reins to tell him to turn so we could go back the way we came. I wasn't ready to go back yet, and I had no intention of riding into view of Reid's sunroom or his stables. But something else caught my attention, and I pulled Khan to a stop.

Once I was on my own feet, I held on to his lead and walked over to where the soil had been torn up. "What the hell?" I reached into my pocket to call London to see if she had any idea, but my cell phone wasn't in my pocket. "Aww, damn it." I had left my phone in the stables. Toeing the chunks of sod that looked to have been cut and then thrown back down, I moved closer and then the earth gave way. What seconds ago had been solid had turned to empty space beneath my foot and I was falling, clumps of dried dirt, plugs of grass, and tiny pebbles falling with me.

I flailed my arms trying to catch hold of something, anything, but my nails dragged down solid soil and dirt rippled underneath me lifting my nails from the beds, the feeling was only one of many excruciating pains triggering my senses. My knees bumped and scraped against the walls, and I tried my best to brace for impact, because there would be one . . . eventually.

When it came, a pain unlike any I'd ever felt before radiated through my shoulder and arm. Heated knives with serrated blades seemed to be carving into the tendons and muscles of my right arm and shoulder. I tried to move it, and nausea rolled through me, making my breakfast churn in my stomach.

I pushed myself up as best as I could with my left arm, but all too soon, my shoulder blades hit the wall behind me. The hole that I'd fallen into was barely wide enough for me to stretch my legs out.

I tried to assess my aches and pains as I rolled my neck. Each movement that pulled on my right shoulder reminded me that something definitely was not right with my arm. Licking my lips, I tasted dirt and salt. I tilted my head back, trying to see how far up the opening was, but all I saw was darkness.

Had I blacked out? I didn't think I had, but it had still been daylight out when I'd fallen. A cold chill swept over me, I think that was what drew my attention to the fact that my toes were ice, my boots were wet, my jeans were soaked, even my shirt and jacket were damp. I wasn't sitting in water, but the ground was thoroughly damp. I reached up and blindingly sharp pain exploded along my arm and down my right side. "Fuck!" I had forgotten about my arm for a brief moment as thoughts of cold occupied my mind, bending forward, I threw up again. The pain was excruciating, radiating through my shoulder, my body, and up to my head, where a dull pounding had begun.

I took several deep breaths and tried to talk myself through the worst of the pain. "Okay, Holland, the right arm is no use." So, I got my legs under me so I could stand, and it took me all of five seconds to realize that I was in a hole, how deep, I had no clue. Using my left arm, I tried to feel around, but I couldn't even feel a ledge or a hold to grab on to.

"Hello? Is anyone out there?" I shouted. "Hello! Help me. Help." My voice started mingling with tears as I continued to yell. "Khan, if you're still out there, go get London. Khan, go." I knew that was wishful thinking. It wasn't as if he were Lassie—hell, I wasn't sure he was even there. He probably went back for dinner. Dinner, my horses, they must be starved.

Sitting back down, I accidentally bumped my right arm and fought the black spots that danced in my vision. I tried to analyze my situation. How was I going to get out of here? Were London and Paris looking for me? They had to be, right? I mean . . . I didn't come up for dinner so they would come looking for me. Unless, of course, they thought I was with the asshole.

As I looked up into the vast darkness, I let the teardrops run freely down my face. Leaning back against my dirt cage, the wet soil of the walls soaking through to my scalp, I closed my eyes and prayed that someone, anyone would find me and that I wouldn't freeze to death in the mean time.

Chapter Fifteen

REID

I was stalling, there was no other way to explain it. I was hanging out around the side of my stables, waiting to see when Holland returned. How dare she not show up to listen to the investigator, how dare she run off and ignore me, what has gotten into the woman?

Only halfheartedly scanning the documents on the clipboard in front of me, I continually looked up and glanced to my left for a sign of her gold braid. At the sound of horse hooves, I finally relaxed and set the clipboard down.

I walked toward the fence to where Khan was standing, alone. "What the hell?" Once I was over the fence, I grabbed hold of his reins and then led him into his stall. "Holland, are you in here?" Scanning the stables and not finding her, I locked up Khan before trudging upstairs and pounding on her door. When there was no answer, I pulled out my phone and shot off a text.

Me: Where are you?

. . .

I waited a minute for the three little bubbles to appear. When they didn't, I typed again.

Me: I found your horse roaming around by himself. I locked him in his stall.

Still no bubbles appeared, and unease kicked up inside me. I wanted to reprimand her for being so irresponsible, but Holland wasn't typically irresponsible—childish, yes, but irresponsible, no.

Girding my loins for what was going to be World War five hundred and something or another, I headed up to the Kellys' main house and knocked.

"Reid, come in," Asher answered as he looked over my shoulder. "Is Holland with you?"

"No. Which is why I'm here, I thought that maybe she was with you all."

"No, we haven't seen her since around three," London added. "Why, what's up?"

"I just found Khan roaming around by himself and locked him in his stall, I knocked on Holland's door but there was no answer, so I came here."

Paris grabbed her phone. "I'm trying to call her."

"I'll get my set of keys to her apartment," London said as she ran off to her apartment.

Paris hung up. "Keeps going to voice mail."

"Paris, will you watch Tera and call Braden's parents for me?" London asked as she handed me the keys.

I didn't wait to find out what Paris said before I was out the door and running. Before I knew it, I was stomping up the stairs, pounding on Holland's door one more time just to be sure before opening the door and searching the tiny apartment. But nothing, she was nowhere to be found.

"Okay, when was the last time you saw Holland?" I turned and faced Braden.

I rubbed my palms against my jeans and told myself that I was being paranoid. My mind was playing through a thousand thoughts of where she could be or what could have happened to her. "Today, I don't know . . . just before five."

"And where was she?"

"She was on her way to my house, but before I could talk to her, she took off on Khan."

"On Khan?" Braden asked.

I nodded.

"Her truck is outside, so we know that she didn't go anywhere. Anything suspicious about Khan?"

I thought about Braden's question. "Yeah, he was still in his tack."

"So she had been riding him."

"Do you think she fell off?" I was ready to go get Nostradamus and search every inch of the property for her if I had to.

"Found her phone." London interrupted us. "It was in the stables." Braden turned to his wife.

"I'm going to go ahead and let the station know. I hate to say this, but I can't do anything as far as county resources until she's been gone for twenty-four hours."

"I don't care about county, I'm looking for her. I'm heading over to my stables to grab a flashlight and saddle up my horse. I'll be back in a few, so if you're ready, you can join me. If not, I'll search by myself." I strode down the stairs, unable to believe that I'd been sitting in my house stewing over Holland's actions when she could have been lying on the ground hurt. God, I would never forgive myself if something happened to her. If someone did something to take away that spark in her eyes or the playfulness in her smile, I would kill them. Holland, even with her forked tongue, was perfect just as she was.

On my way to my stables, I called Syd.

"Hey, what's up?"

"Get Nostradamus saddled for me, quick please."

"Got it." Syd hung up, and I slid my phone into my pocket. I ran the last few hundred feet to the fence and then jumped over it. Rounding the corner, I pulled open the door and moved straight to Hightower.

"Okay, buddy, I need you. It's your turn to show me what kind of bond you've formed with Holland." I grabbed a bit and a lead rein from the wall and then moved into Hightower's stall. He wasn't pleased with me, but I wanted to find Holland more than I wanted to deal with his emotions.

"What's going on?" Syd asked as he walked Nostradamus out and into the center row.

"Holland is missing. No one has seen her since around five when I saw her on Khan. I found him about twenty minutes ago wandering the field still in his tack."

"What can I do to help?"

"You can go grab a light and search around the perimeter of my house. Then stay close just in case she shows up here."

I handed Syd Hightower's lead and then climbed up on Nostradamus, once settled, I took the lead back and wrapped it around my hand.

"Let me know if you hear anything, that girl is a sweetie," Syd hollered as he moved to saddle up another horse.

"Will do." I rode out, with Hightower at my side. When I approached the Kellys' stables, I was surprised by the small group of people who had gathered. There was a rescue truck, two deputy cars, several pickup trucks, and a few Jeeps.

"You've brought Hightower," Ellie exclaimed.

"Yeah, have you bonded with him as well?"

"Ever since Holland started, he lets me."

"Great, you take him." I handed her the lead. "I didn't saddle him because I didn't know anyone else could handle him."

"We have a light saddle that she can use," London offered as tears ran unchecked down her cheeks.

"Come on, Ellie, I'll help you find it," Asher said.

"Here's how we will run things." Braden had assumed lead and was directing everyone. "Ben"—he pointed to the fireman—"will be here as home base since he has the medic vehicle. Marcus, if you'll drive your Jeep and use your spotlights, and David," Braden said to the other deputy, "will use his Explorer with its spotlights. We will divide into two groups, you will stay in front of the vehicles and fan out so that you are covering more area. She may be hurt or unconscious, so pay attention." Braden turned his focus to me. "Reid, is anyone at your place?"

"My stable manager knows what's going on and is on the lookout, he'll notify me if she shows up there."

"Great. Asher and Marcus's mother is also looking out for her. My parents are here, one at the big house and one at my home just in case she shows up at either place."

My mind was whirling with a million and one horrible scenarios. What if she wasn't on the property at all? With each image that flashed in front of my eyes, a lump grew in my throat that made it almost impossible to swallow.

"Are you okay?" Ellie asked as she sidled up next to me.

"Yeah. Just worried for her."

Ellie reached out and grabbed hold of my hand and gave me a knowing look. "We'll find her, I promise. She's had an accident, that's all. I feel it. We will find her—"

"Let's roll!" Braden hollered. "Stay in contact with each other. Call London or me if you see anything."

We divided into two groups, and Braden climbed onto

Khan, hoping that the horse could lead them back to where they last were. So, I made sure that Ellie stayed with me, I wanted Hightower there. It ended up being Ellie, Asher, and myself riding in front of David's sheriff's truck. While London, Paris, and Braden rode in front of Marcus, since they wanted a sheriff on both sides.

Both groups headed out with London's group veering right and our group going left. Asher moved toward the fence, Ellie stayed in the middle, and I took the right part of our first sweep. We worked our way away from the stables. With four hundred acres to cover, we would be here through morning. But if that didn't pan out, there was still my land and Asher's mother's. It could take another twenty-four hours if we went non-stop.

I scanned the ground, to the left and right of me. David had his spotlights on top of his sheriff's truck with the light bar totally illuminated, I could see a good distance in front of me.

I hadn't told Holland that I had a crush on her. Jesus Christ, crush? How old was I? But, what else was it? I liked her, and I have liked her for a while. God, after our night, I hadn't been able to get her out of my mind, and the thought of not being able to have that again made it hard to breathe.

The first time I saw her, she was extending her heels when she rode, and I mentioned it to her and she lost her mind. Shaking my head at the memory, another flashed front and center, it was the first time I had gone over to the Kellys' and she had lost her mind and had called me an asshole in front of everyone. I couldn't lose that—the world couldn't lose that fire, and I needed her to spar with. She made my day brighter. I wouldn't know how to start my day without seeing her out riding.

"Holland!" I hollered, I was the first one to break the silent night sky. I glanced over to find Ellie watching me. A second later she hollered, and a second after that, Asher did as well. Before I knew it we were each hollering, taking turns and then waiting a little bit to see if she responded.

"Whoa. Calm down, Hightower." Ellie leaned forward and patted Hightower's neck. He lifted his front feet again. "Reid, something is wrong."

I pulled Nostradamus over and tried to help soothe Hightower, but he was having none of it. "He senses something. Asher, call Braden. I want to see if Khan can help. Ellie, dismount and take Nostradamus." I jumped down and handed her the reins then walking with Hightower by the lead, I turned on my flashlight and began combing the area on foot.

"Holland. Holland, can you hear me?" I walked, searching to my right and left. Hightower pulled a little bit and pranced. "Okay, buddy, what's going on?"

"He began acting up when we started calling her name, could it be that he just doesn't like the noise?" Asher asked as he rode up behind me.

"No, Hightower is used to loud noises from the race circuit, I seriously doubt that would spook him."

I saw lights in the distance coming from two areas, one was obviously Marcus and the other was coming from the direction we had left. "Do we know who that is?" I asked.

"It's Ben. Braden called him to head this way because if we find her then he'll be ready."

London, Paris, and Braden all raced up at the same time. "Tell me exactly what happened?"

I turned to face Braden as my sister moved over to Marcus, who grabbed her hand up in his. The sight of that crushed me because I wanted that with Holland. "The more we move in this direction the more he's acting up. I want to see if Khan goes in this direction. Ellie, why don't you get back on Hightower and you and Braden go off and see if the horses lead you anywhere, we'll be right behind you both."

Ellie looked over to Braden, who nodded. We exchanged horses once again. "Here take this, you'll need it." I handed her my flashlight. "Please."

"I will. I promise." My sister knew what I meant. My one-word plea and she totally knew everything.

I climbed back on Nostradamus as Braden and Ellie took off, Marcus following them. The rest of us moved a bit slower, still fanning out and combing the area. Except for the bouncing of the flashlight in the distance, I could no longer see Ellie or Braden, they were too far ahead of us. For hours we searched, and I never once let that speck of light in front of us get out of sight. As the sky darkened to the inky black of pre-dawn, my heart sank lower.

London's phone rang. "It's Braden."

She must have pressed speakerphone. "Come to the far corner toward Reid's property but move along the fence line, I think we've found her."

It was all we needed to hear before we all took off. It was at that moment that I realized that I would rather fight with Holland Kelly than be with anyone else, it sounded all kinds of messed up, but I didn't care.

"Slow down, watch your step!" Braden yelled when I got close to them. I slowed Nostradamus to a trot because even though I couldn't see much, he had a great sense of danger and I was relying on him.

"What's going on?" But no one had to answer my question instead they both moved their flashlights toward the hole. "It that an old well?" It was hard to see since it was so dark.

"I doubt it since it appears to just be dirt. There doesn't look to be any lining not even wood," Braden answered. The rest of the group arrived, but David, Marcus, and Sam stayed on the outskirts. "I asked them to stay back, I'm not sure whether this is part of a sinkhole, although I don't think it is since it looks to be perfectly shaped, but it's so dark that I just can't be sure. I don't trust the ground stability."

I was glad that he was thinking clearly because all I wanted to do was rappel down that hole and see if she was down there.

"We've hollered but there is no answer and our lights aren't strong enough to see what's down there," Braden explained. "We're going to try some of the emergency lights that we have."

I turned to see Ben and David each carrying a different style of high-beam light. Paris, London, and Ellie were all leaning toward the edge and shouting Holland's name.

"Come away from there," Braden and Asher reprimanded their wives.

"What? It's okay for you to risk your life?" London asked. "That's my sister."

"Yeah, and she's my sister-in-law, but I won't be of any help to anyone if you fall down there. I need to keep a level head. Please," Braden pleaded, and London stepped back, pulling Paris with her.

Running a portable inverter connected via a long exten-sion cord back to the rescue truck, Ben and Braden powered on the first light. The area lit up like Disney World.

I shielded my eyes from the brightness. "Reid, we will hold this but since we are so close we won't be able to see anything, can you and Asher try?"

"Of course." I moved toward the ledge and laid flat on my stomach, not caring that the cold damp ground soaked through to my skin. The light moved, the beam directed down, and it took several seconds for my eyes to adjust enough for me to make out anything at the bottom. "I see her," Asher and I both said in unison.

"Is she alive?" London asked. Paris let out a heart-wrenching sob.

"Help." I think she said yes but it was so faint, it was actually more muffled. So I tried again.

"Holland, can you hear me? Please move, a leg, an arm, anything."

"Is she moving?" London raced over to me.

"Jesus Christ, London, step back and give her a second," Braden barked.

"Holland, come on, Tiger, please move something." While I was waiting on Holland to answer my request, my brain was registering that Braden was giving orders to David. Something about a winch, safety harness, tandem straps, body camera.

That's when I saw it, her legs slowly extending. "She moved. She fucking moved. She's trying to sit up." I hollered to the group. "That's it, just be careful, we're going to get you out of there, I promise."

Marcus and Asher moved to take Ben and Braden's places holding the light so that the two of them could get the rescue operation in full gear.

"Here." Braden knelt by me and handed me a radio that was tethered to a rope. "I put it on a channel C-seventeen." He handed me the rope, and I slowly started easing it down as Braden spoke the entire time.

"Holland, this is Braden. Take the radio. Leave it tied. Press the button on the side and talk to me. Holland, this is Braden, grab ahold of the radio. Leave it tied. Press the button on the side and talk to me." He repeated the same thing over and over until, the radio let out a crackling sound a second before Holland's voice came over the air.

"Hey. You found me."

I hadn't realized how long I had been holding my breath until that moment. The sound of her voice filled me with a jumble of thoughts, gratitude, and anxiety, but most of all, there was the desire for time to hurry the fuck up so I could get her out of that hole and into my arms.

"Of course, we found you. Listen to me. I need you to tell me if there is any slack in the rope."

"Yes."

"Okay, we're going to pull some back up, tell me when that slack is gone." Braden gave me a nod, and I started slowly easing some of the rope back up.

"Okay, stop." Holland's voice was weak.

I turned to Braden to see what was going on. But David had the other end of the rope and was straightening it out. Then with a tape measure, he was measuring off segments. "There are about eleven feet left," he called out.

"Holland is twenty-four feet down," Braden exclaimed. I felt guilty for letting everyone else work, but I didn't want to take my eyes off her. "Here, Reid, take my radio." I grabbed it from Braden and tuned out everything but the girl on the end of the line.

I pressed the button and began talking, "Hey, Tiger."

"Reid, is Khan okay?"

"He's fine. You're going to see him very soon."

A sob broke from her and I sucked in my breath at the sound of her pain. "I'm hungry."

"What's your favorite thing to eat?"

"Pancakes."

"Pancakes?" I chuckled. "More than steak or pizza?"

"Yeah, pancakes. I love pancakes."

"Then I'll make you pancakes as soon as you're safe."

"Reid?"

"Yes, sweetheart?"

"I'm hurt, I can't move my arm." Holland stopped and for the first time I really noticed that they sounded labored.

I hollered out to whoever was listening, "Sounds like she

may have broken a rib or two, her breathing is labored." Then I returned to Holland. "I was mad at you."

"You were?"

"Yeah, I thought you stood me up."

Holland let out a small laugh. "You feel guilty, huh?"

"Leave it to you, you're in a hole and probably trying to figure out how to get the upper hand." I paused for a second to see if she'd laugh. "Tiger, I promise that we'll find who left this hole, I'll make them pay."

"I just want to get warm."

"I know, honey, we're going to get you out of there real quick and get you warmed up. Holland, I'm going to take care of you, I promise."

"Will you just hold me? I'm so cold."

There were a few seconds of silence, and my finger was getting ready to press the button when the line crackled and she whispered, "Reid?"

"Yes."

"How am I going to get out of here?"

"I'm going to come down and get you." I wasn't sure what they were planning on doing, but if anyone was going down to get her, it was going to be me. I needed her in my arms, and I needed to know that she was safe.

Chapter Sixteen

REID

It took about an hour for the troops to rally and for everyone to return. Spotlights were propped up around the area, vehicle lights were pointing toward the center, and now we were deciding the best mode of rescue.

"She says her right arm hurts, and she is having a hard time breathing, maybe a broken rib or two. She won't be able to hold on to anything, so I need to go down to get her."

"Hold on, Reid, we need to think about this, you're a big guy, I'm not sure there will be enough room for you to move around."

That was completely unacceptable. Without dropping my glare from Brandon, I grabbed the radio. "Holland, how much room is down there with you? Would I fit?"

"I don't think so. It's small." Holland had finally pushed herself up and stuck out her left arm. "I'm touching the sides."

"See . . . I don't think you'll have freedom of movement, and even if you do get down there, there is no way you'll get back up with her in your arms."

It irked me, but I knew that he was right. There was no

way. I turned to face Ellie and had to force back the burn of emotion behind my eyes. My sister, who had always meant the world to me, knew what I was about to ask before I asked it, but still, I whispered, "Please. I can't . . ."

For several seconds, Ellie didn't say a word, then slowly she shut her eyes as in a silent prayer. "You don't have to say anything, I know. I'll get her out safe."

"I'm also worried about you."

"Oh, shush." Ellie hit my arm, and our gentle moment was broken and back to the normal sibling banter. She stepped over to where Braden and Ben were standing with a few other deputies and firemen and Marcus wrapped an arm around her and tucked her close to his side.

I tried to keep one eye on Ellie as they harnessed her up and walked her through what to do as well as watch Holland to make sure she was hanging in there. She was leaning against the wall of the hole, her legs were outstretched, picking up the radio again, I spoke. "Holland, stay awake for me. We're coming down now."

She lifted the radio. "I'm so cold."

"I know, honey. I promise, just a few more minutes." I glanced over to Ben, who had several silver foiled blankets and a few large packets that looked like pillows sitting on a stretcher.

"Reid, keep talking to Holland, Ellie, you keep talking as you descend. Once down there, talk us through what you are doing. Do you get me?" Braden asked and Ellie nodded as Ben double-checked the straps on her harness then wrapped Velcro bands around her wrist.

"Once you have her, fold your arms over each other and the Velcro will help you keep your hold. Finally, remember, before you tell us to start pulling you up, squat, have Holland wrap her legs around you, face-to-face. Move this strap, the strap is very important"—he tugged on a loose strap that hung at the back of her like a swing—"secure it under your thighs, and it will help form a seat on the way up so you aren't having to hold all of Holland's weight. I doubt that she'll have any strength to help you."

Ellie nodded.

"Be careful of her ribs, don't want to puncture a lung, and watch out for her right arm."

"Got it." Ellie gave a thumbs-up.

"Holland, are you ready?" I asked into the radio.

"Yes, so ready."

"Okay, we're coming down." Ellie moved to the hole and slowly the men fed the rope down and Ellie using her feet, kept herself straight and walked down the wall. "Do you see Ellie?"

"It's Ellie? I thought you were coming."

Her words crushed me. "I was too big."

Holland chuckled. "Don't make me laugh, it hurts to laugh."

"I'm sorry, I don't want you to hurt."

"Reid?"

"Yes?"

"I'm sorry about being mean to you. I'm sorry about throwing manure on your house and about locking you out. I'm sorry about mooning you and flipping you off."

I heard Braden and Marcus laughing.

Paris was laughing and still crying, "You know that, once she feels better, she will forget apologizing and go back to doing all of those things again, don't you?"

"I hope so." I truly did. I loved our banter.

"She's almost here. I hear her talking." Holland's words were still so weak.

"She has a radio as well and is talking to Braden."

"They're laughing."

"Yeah, they think it's funny that you threw shit at my

house. Should I tell them that you tried to throw it at me as well?"

"I said I was sorry. Hey, she's here. She said to pull the radio up."

I glanced over at Braden, and he nodded. I hated not having that contact with Holland. "Okay, do as Ellie says, and I'll be up here waiting for you." Holland didn't say anything else, and I started pulling the radio up. When it was in my hands, I moved over to the guys and waited for word from Ellie.

"I have the five-point harness on her. I'm connecting her harness to mine now." Ellie was silent for a few seconds. "I'm attaching her to the rope. I'm squatting and moving the straps underneath me." Ellie was talking us through just as Ben had asked. I looked over and he was mimicking her movements, his way of making sure that no step was left undone. "She is wrapping her legs around me, and I've fastened my wrists. We're ready."

Ben spoke into the radio that connected to Ellie. "Holland, are you ready?"

Holland's voice so much softer than Ellie's. "Yes."

The men started pulling, and the winch started slowly cranking.

"Reid, take this." Ben threw me a foil blanket and one of the pillow packs. "It's a heat blanket. As soon as you see her, pop that button on the side, then once she is out of the hole, peel the corners of the pack apart and pull the blanket out, wrap it around her. Lay the foil shock blanket over it, it will help hold the heat in."

I nodded and moved toward the opening, watching, my heart pounding with each passing second.

"I've got you, we're almost there." Ellie's soothing words repeated over and over across the air. "We've been so worried.

I'm so glad you're okay. You should see Reid, I've never seen him so distraught."

My sister could say anything she wanted to make Holland feel better or to distract her from whatever pain she was in.

When their heads appeared above the hole, I pulled the blanket out and move toward Holland, wrapping her in warmth. When she was unhooked, I tried hard not to hurt her as I wrapped her in the heat blankets and lowered my mouth to hers. "Thank god, thank god."

The stretcher had been moved behind her, and Holland was eased backward. Ben quickly removed the harness. Ben and the paramedic took over and worked as they carried the stretcher toward the rescue truck. "Who's coming with her?"

I turned to London and Paris, pleading for them to let me.

London nodded. "We'll be right behind you."

"Ellie, will you take Nostradamus back?"

"Of course, just go."

By the time I jumped into the back of the rescue truck, Ben already had an IV in Holland, oxygen going, and a pulse-ox running. "Looks like her right shoulder is dislocated. May be some broken ribs, her right ankle also sustained some damage, but we won't know how bad until we get some X-rays done."

I grabbed hold of Holland's hand and didn't let go. When we pulled in front of the ER, the back doors opened and then Ben and one of the other men had Holland out and rolling through the doors, I followed, never letting go. Our eyes were locked, and a single tear ran down her face.

"It's okay, I'm not going anywhere."

"Hi, who do we have here?" a male nurse greeted us. Ben answered his questions and handed over the forms he had filled out on our way here. The nurse quickly read over them.

"Hi, Holland, I'm Keith. On a scale of one to ten, how is your pain right now?"

"Eleven."

"We're going to get you moved into a room and get some X-rays. Let's get you moved into room nine, okay?" He pointed to a hospital bed against the wall.

She nodded, and after a few minutes, they had her settled in the hospital bed and the paramedics were moving out.

"Holland, we're going to go." Ben placed a hand on Holland's head. "I'll call your sisters tomorrow and check in on you, okay?"

"Thanks, Ben."

"Thank you," I said before shaking his hand.

"We need to get her into this gown." Keith grabbed a faded, pale blue ugly piece of fabric. "Holland, do you need help?"

"I don't know."

"I'll help." I was being stupid, I knew I was, but I wasn't sure that I wanted this guy helping her undress. "I'll probably need to cut her shirt off. Do you have scissors?" Keith reached into a drawer and pulled out a pair of blunt tip medical shears and set them on a tray along with a plastic bag.

"I'll be back in a few minutes. Holler if you need help." Keith left and pulled the curtain closed behind him.

"Okay, Tiger, let's get you changed."

I pulled back the covers and began with her jeans. They were caked with mud, and I had to be careful as I worked them over her injured ankle, but I eventually got them off her.

"Just throw those away."

I pressed on the garbage can and opened the lid dropping the jeans inside. Then moving to her shirt I tried to examine the best way to do it. "I don't want to hurt you. I'm going to cut your shirt on your right side and then try to peel it off you, okay?"

Holland nodded.

As I started to move the fabric away, I finally saw the bruises that covered her sides. Her shoulder was hanging lower than the rest of her torso. Yep, I'd seen this many times when I had played football; she had dislocated her shoulder. No wonder she was in so much pain.

"You really did a number. No wonder you're hurting so bad."

"Well, you know I never do anything halfway."

"No. No, you don't." I let out a pained chuckle and pulled the hospital gown around her. "The good thing is that, if it is just dislocated, once they get it set, it will start feeling better almost right away."

"Are you dressed?" Keith asked from the other side of the curtain.

"Yes."

"Holland, X-ray will be here in a few minutes, the doctor has ordered them to take images of your chest, ribs, shoulder, and ankle. He's also ordered an ultrasound and a CT."

"Why an ultrasound? I'm not pregnant."

"No, it lets us know that you didn't injure anything in your abdomen."

My phone rang, and I looked down to see that Braden was calling. "Hello?"

"We're here, where are you?"

"We're back in the ER, room nine."

"Thanks." Braden disconnected.

"Your sisters are here," I said and squeezed her hand. Holland's face lit up.

I turned at the sound of chatter and several pairs of shoes hurrying along the travertine tile. Keith stuck his head out but then stepped out of the way.

"Okay, there are a lot of you, decide who is staying and the majority of you will need to go out to the waiting room and sit."

"Give them a minute, okay?" I asked.

Keith gave me a head nod. "X-ray will be here any minute." He stepped out.

"Oh, Holland." Paris leaned in. "I brought you a change of clothes."

"Tell me there are underwear in there."

"I brought five pairs."

"Thank god."

Holland spoke to her sisters while Brandon and I stepped out so she could finish changing.

"Here are your keys. Asher drove it down, it's parked just outside the doors and to the right."

"Thank you."

"What are they saying?"

"Nothing yet, she hasn't seen a doctor yet, and we're waiting on X-ray."

"Do we have any idea about that hole?" Asher asked.

"It's too perfect, this was mechanically dug," Braden pointed out. "Someone had to have brought a Ditch Witch, some form of directional drill, or an auger back here. I have David and another deputy setting up a perimeter and forensics is on their way. A piece of equipment that large had to leave some tracks."

"I think it was Holbrook." I was pacing as I said it because the information was clicking into place too fast for me to stay still.

"The land developer, why?"

"Apparently, someone has been doing soil tests on our land, and one of those tests required digging up a large amount of soil to be tested. I don't know for sure that it was him, but who else could it have been?"

"What could he possibly be looking for?"

"Phosphate. Here is why I believe it is Holbrook though." Braden and Asher stopped dividing their attention between me and the rest of chaos going on. Both of them turned to me, they were focused. "For eminent domain, land surveys would need to have been completed but none have been done, the most recent anyone has was mine when I purchased my property. But there are Sustainable Management surveys, testing for sustainable resources such as phosphate."

"If he had anything to do with this, I'll have his ass," Braden said, steam practically rising from him.

"You and me both."

Chapter Seventeen

HOLLAND

It was crazy, one of my sisters had spent practically every minute with me over the past twenty-four hours. But Reid never left me, not once.

"All right, Holland, we are letting you go. Here are your instructions and your prescriptions. If you should notice abnormal swelling or discoloration, if your pain intensifies or you get a fever, please come back. Check up with your primary physician." I nodded to the nurse who had been taking care of me since I'd been admitted. She was nice, but I was ready to get the hell out of here. "Avoid any heavy lifting, climbing stairs, or physical exertion for the next four weeks. Give your ribs time to heal." I nodded even though she'd told me that four times already. "You're all set."

Reid helped me over to the wheelchair.

"I'm going down to get the truck. I'll meet you out front." Reid leaned down and placed a kiss on my head before taking off.

"My, he sure is a looker," the nurse said once he was out of earshot.

I didn't respond as she rolled me down the long hallway

that led to the parking lot. When the double doors slid open, Reid was already waiting with the passenger door open. After he helped me in and I got fastened, I blurted out what had been on my mind. "I want to go to my house."

"You can't do stairs."

"Then take me to the big house."

"Paris and Asher are still newlyweds. Besides, I want to take care of you."

I wasn't sure how to respond to that, and for a minute, I didn't. Then I realized how ridiculous I was being and gave in. "Thank you, I appreciate it I really do but I think it is best for me to go to my family."

Reid reached over and took hold of my left hand lightly squeezing it. "Why?"

I bit my lower lip and thought how to say this. How do I tell him that seeing him bring other girls around would . . . well, I don't know what it would do, I just know that I wouldn't like it.

"Okay, but first answer one thing that has been bothering me."

"What?"

"Why did you run?"

"Run?" I was a horrible actress, and I knew there was no way he was going to believe my stupid act.

"Yeah . . . on Khan, the day you were supposed to come to my house, the day you fell into the hole and got hurt. You ran away and I hollered for you."

"I . . . I didn't want to interrupt you."

"What? I invited you over so you could join us."

"Umm, that didn't really work for me." He and I were obviously talking about two different things.

"Will you just spit it out?"

"I saw you, okay? I saw you and her on your front porch. The way you looked at her—"

"You're nuts. I'm not sure what you saw, but it wasn't anything like you're thinking. The PI is from my hometown and we grew up together, that's all. The only person I have feelings for is you. I've been trying to get you to see that but you're too damn stubborn to see it."

Every hair on my body stood on end. Heat radiated over my skin, and I wanted to kill him.

"I'm too stubborn?" I yanked my hand back from him, the movement sent pain shooting through me.

"Holland, will you stop?"

"No."

"You've been all sweet the last few days and with the flip of a switch you are in full bitch mode. What's going on? Do you not feel the same for me?"

"No. I do not." The words were a lie, but I refused to let him get the upper hand.

"Well, then that changes everything a bit. Will you please still come to my house so I can take care of you? Your sisters will have extra work with the stables, and I already told them that I was bringing you to my house. Plus, we have stuff to go over concerning Holbrook."

"Please, Reid, I just want to be with my sisters."

"Christ, Holland, do you despise being in my company that much? What? You were fine leaning on me the last two days, but now that you're out, you don't need me? I don't understand you. One second you're hot, and the next, you're cold."

I didn't answer him because he was turning on the road to my house. He slowed down and tried to avoid the ruts in the road and keep the jostling to a minimum.

When he pulled in front of my house, I tried to open my door. "Stop. I'll come around." He did, and having him sweep me in his arms tore at my heart. As he carried me up the few steps of the front porch, I could feel his eyes boring into me, and I tried to avoid his stare. The front door opened, London and Paris were there to greet me.

"Holland, we're so happy to see you." Paris stepped back so Reid could enter, me still cradled in his arms.

"Sorry, she doesn't want to come to my house and ordered me to bring her here."

"Bring her back here." London led the way to my old bedroom. Reid set me down. "We took a bunch of her stuff over to your house and set it up in your downstairs bedroom—"

"No worries, I'll get it back to you all. I'm meeting with the investigator tomorrow, and, if you don't mind, I'd like to bring her here so you all can hear whatever she has to say, I think Braden should be in on this. I'll bring Holland's stuff then as well."

"Okay, I'll give him a call," London said as she left the room.

"Can't you meet her at your house?"

"What's gotten into you? You were such an integral part of this fight and standing up against Holbrook, and now it's as if you don't care."

"Nothing is wrong with me, I'm just tired."

"Bullshit. You're running away. You're picking up your toys and going home, just like a spoiled little brat."

"Spoiled? I'm not spoiled! You're spoiled. Mr. High and Mighty." I deepened my voice, "Oh, look at me, I know all about Thoroughbreds, my family has been involved in racing for years."

"I don't talk like that."

But I wasn't finished. "Poor little country girl, old horse, old saddle, good god, does anyone actually ride that way anymore? A real lady would ride side saddle."

"Women do not ride side saddle anymore, you're being

overly dramatic. I've never once thought you were a poor country girl. A bratty one, yes. Now tell me what is wrong."

"Excuse me, but last I checked, I wasn't wearing a dog collar and you weren't my owner, so stop barking orders at me. Get out."

Reid cupped his forehead, his index finger pressing on one temple and his thumb pressing on the other. It was a gesture that I had seen my father make a thousand times when he was at his limit with us. "I'm done." Reid held his hands up in the air. "I've been trying to show you that I like you, but that obviously doesn't matter. You are only ever going to find the bad in people. You know what, Holland, keep it up, and you will find yourself old, alone, and bitter."

"Humph."

"Woman . . . never mind. You need to get your rest. I'm glad that we found you and you're doing okay." Reid bent and cupped my cheek and something inside me wanted to beg him not to leave, don't go, ask for his forgiveness. But I couldn't bring myself to do it, instead I turned my head and watched him walk out of my childhood bedroom.

London swept in after Reid left. "Holland, how could you just let him leave? You two have been playing this enemy-to-lovers dance for almost two years. You have to be blind not to see that you just hurt him and that you're being too stubborn to believe that he cares about you and you care about him. Or do I have this all wrong and you truly feel nothing for him?"

Tears rolled down my cheeks, and I reached up to wipe them away. "No, that isn't it. I do like him . . . a lot. I messed up, okay?"

"Then why didn't you say anything kind?"

"You didn't see him or the way he looked at the investigator, London. She was perfect."

"So? Who cares if she was perfect? Clearly, she wasn't perfect for Reid, and isn't he the one who matters?"

"But it was more than that, you should have seen her, the way she stood, her hair, everything just seemed so prim and proper."

"Not if she's a private investigator. She was probably just wearing her professional attire since she was meeting Reid. But you and I both know that isn't the kind of man Reid is, none of those things are practical not with the kind of life he wants. My god, look at his sister, he loves her and she is usually covered in dog hair, never in high heels or fancy clothes."

"But—"

"No buts, you were wrong."

"It seems like it is the story of my life. I can't believe I let my emotions rule me again, if I had slowed down just a little and thought about this maybe I wouldn't be here." I waved my left hand over the bed. "This is all my fault, falling in the hole, leaving my phone, everything. I'm such a fuck up." My tears were rolling down my face faster.

London moved toward the door. "Get some sleep, holler if you need anything and we'll get it for you. I'll be back in a little while to check on you. Just rest." London walked out and closed the door behind her.

I let the rest of the tears fall.

———

I woke the next morning and the pain hadn't lessened. Not just my ribs, sure they hurt, but I had expected this since I was warned that the third day was the worst, but I was talking about the pain in my chest. I hadn't seen or heard from Reid since yesterday when he dropped me off.

I cringed as I moved at the pace of a snail, fumbling to sit up and try to pull socks on. Last night, it took me over two hours just to take a shower, and finally Paris came in and washed my hair. I eventually made it to the dresser mirror and groaned. I looked like someone had just dug me up from a cemetery. I was pale, my hair was flat, and I had dark shadows under my eyes. Maybe I should be glad that Reid hadn't been back to see me.

Glancing down at my sweatpants and T-shirt that I had slept in, I decided that I would stay in those since I was too sore to change. Making my way to the bathroom to brush my teeth was going to be hard enough. I wasn't going to add changing my clothing on top of it.

When I was finally ready, I made my way to the living room and smiled at my niece, Tera, who was in a bouncy seat. "Morning, boo." I blew her a kiss.

"Have a seat, and I'll bring you a bowl of grits." Paris moved to the stove, and I spent the next few minutes trying to lower myself into the oversized recliner. "Reid is going to be here in a bit with that investigator, and Braden is going to meet them here. Are you up to listening in?" she asked as she handed me the warm bowl.

"Have to be."

"You sure? If not, London or I can take notes for you."

"Thanks but no, I need to woman-up and do this myself. This is my battle I'm fighting. Will I have time to go out to the stables?"

"Ha ha, very funny. There's no way you're going to the stables like that. I doubt you could make it that far."

"But my horses—"

Paris held up one hand and silenced me. "The horses are fine and are being taken care of. Do you seriously think that Asher would let anything happen to them?" Paris was right, so I dropped my eyes back to my bowl. "You finish up, I'm going to go grab a brush and hair tie so that I can help you with that rat's nest on your head."

I smiled at Tera, who had no worries in the world except

whether or not someone would change her diaper or give her food. The amount of my childhood I'd wasted wishing that I was grown-up and trying to be a grown-up faster than I should was absurd. It was more absurd that I was a grown-up and couldn't seem to actually act like one.

"Turn your head," Paris said as she dragged the paddle brush through my hair. I loved the way her fingers felt as they slid across my scalp, pulling and tugging the strands as she wove my hair into a French braid. She tied it off with a band. "Look at me." I did as ordered. She opened her tube of concealer and dabbed the creamy liquid under my eyes. "Won't totally get rid of the circles, but it should help." When she was finished massaging the cover-up into my skin, she stepped back and examined me. "Better. You still look like you fell down a twenty-five foot hole, broke two ribs, dislocated your shoulder, and twisted your ankle, but at least now you look like you're going to survive."

Chapter Eighteen

HOLLAND

The front door opened, and I turned to see Braden in his sheriff's uniform walk in. Reid and the raven-haired woman were right behind him.

It wasn't what it seemed, it wasn't what it seemed. I kept saying those words over and over in my mind.

"Are you okay?" Paris whispered.

I nodded because, for some reason, I wasn't able to speak. Paris bent and rubbed one hand over mine. "Are you in pain?"

Yes, but not the kind of pain that medicine would help, I didn't think there was medicine for a broken heart. "No, I'm fine, really."

"Then you might want to let loose the death grip that you have on the arm of the chair. I wouldn't be shocked if someone asks you if you need an Ex-Lax if you keep this up."

I stuck out my tongue since it was too much trouble to raise my middle finger, but I did let go of my grip.

"Paris, Holland, I'd like you to meet Brandy Lakote, she's the investigator who has been researching Johnson Holbrook for us."

"Hello," Paris greeted her, always so friendly to everyone.

I, on the other hand, not so much. I gave her a nod.

"I'm so sorry to hear what happened to you. Besides being hurt, I'm sure that you must have been frightened—I know I would have been. Well, you look amazing for what you've been through. I hope that I'll be able to relieve some stress with some of the information that I have." Okay, the woman was friendly, but that didn't mean I had to be best buddies with her. "Where would you like me to sit?" She asked the question so anyone could answer, but her eyes were on me. I glanced to Paris since technically this was her home.

"Wherever is fine. How about the couch so that Holland doesn't have to move again?"

"Perfect."

London came in, and Braden grabbed another chair from the kitchen. I watched as my family, ever conscious of my feelings, moved like it had been preplanned. Paris sat next to Brandy. Braden handed Reid the chair, which he set close to me. And Braden and London moved to the loveseat. I glanced over and saw Reid grinning at them as well. He knew the kind of games my family played, well, he'd been part of it when we played them with London and with Paris so I have no clue why I was shocked.

Brandy pulled out a laptop and then several printed documents. She handed Reid a copy, and he passed them to Braden.

"Let's discuss the hole. It appears as if this particular hole has been there for several months. Braden, that information you gave Reid about the tire tracks was extremely helpful and led me to the type of equipment used, without it, we still might not have the most incriminating evidence of all. First, let me tell you that the tires are Nokian Mine, they are made specifically for drill rigs, which let me know that the hole was actually dug by a well drilling rig."

"Who, how?" Paris, London, and I questioned at the same time.

"I'm getting to that." Brandy held up one finger. "Once I figured out the equipment, I started contacting companies that drilled wells until I found the one." Brandy took several pieces of paper that were stapled together off the tall stack she had set out and passed it around. When it got to me, I saw that it was a contract for hire to Frampton Wells, including the proposal, and receipt upon completion. "He was hired and told it was to be a shallow well only to supply water to that back quadrant of land. But the owner never had the well finished, and of course, that seemed odd to them, but the bill was paid, so they let it go."

"There's no name on this contract, just our address. Who hired them?"

"That took a little more digging," Brandy explained. "They keep their clients information private, but they don't hide the invoice numbers. I just sat in the office and patiently waited to speak to Mr. Frampton and when the secretary needed to take a potty break, I entered the invoice number, and voila." Brandy pulled out a photo of a computer screen that showed the invoice she was talking about. We could all see the customer name. Johnson Holbrook. "It is the only thing we have that actually has his name, but it's also the most important thing since the geophysicist was brought out to test that hole."

"That son of a bitch," I hissed.

"Why our land? What made him choose this area?" London asked.

"It seems that for the last several years, Lake Harney has had some serious algae issues, as well as a few new homes in Seminole Woods subdivision have built swimming pools and are experiencing abnormal algae issues as well. All of these reports of course are documented with the county."

"What does algae growth have to do with my property? Or any of the properties they want to buy?"

"Holbrook had been working with a geophysicist who had actually accompanied him out to several of the properties. According to him, it's a nutrient source for algae and also an indication that an area is rich with phosphate. " Brandy took a few more pages from her stack and passed them around. They were a variety of scientific tests including the chemical formula PO_4^{3-}. I wracked my brain to try to remember the chemical formula chart from back in high school. O was easy, that was oxygen, but was P phosphorus or phosphoric acid? Crap. I really should have paid more attention. I finally gave up and asked, hoping someone had paid attention in chemistry. "Is PO_4^{3-} the chemical compound for phosphate?"

Brandy must have been the only one or she had Googled it earlier. "Yes it is. You see, to Holbrook, all of those algae reports meant that there was phosphate. Many of the land samples were done with simple surface magnetic testing, but it seems that the Kellys' land gave some astronomical numbers, which is what led him to do a drilling sample."

"So . . . if I'm reading this right, they found phosphates on our property?"

"They did. But unless you want to turn your yard into a mine, there's little that can be done since you need to dig deep to get it."

"I understand the importance of phosphate—hello, we're ranchers, after all. I'm just not willing to ruin our property to get it." This aggravated me because phosphates were needed, without them there would be no way to supply enough food for the world, it is what made fertilizer work and grow vegetables and fruits as well as grass and hay feed. "But why would a land developer be interested?"

"I have two theories." Brandy pulled out another packet of paper. "Minute Maid—"

"As in orange juice?"

"That's the one, has been selling their land in Polk County, which is just an hour and a half from here. As you know, that area is theme park central, you have Disney on one side and then Legoland right at the back of their property. With these came a rise in tourists which also mean a rise in traffic, congestion, and pollution. The EPA has documented the decline in soil nutrient tests. An area like this that is land locked may be worth top dollar to a big company grower if the soil were rich in nutrients."

"What's your other theory?" I asked.

"Are you familiar with Bone Valley?" Brandy asked. I shook my head. "It is the major phosphate mining area of Florida, it has been in operation since the late nineteenth century. It seems that people are offering top dollar for large parcels of land with a minimum of twenty-five thousand acres." Brandy opened an aerial map. "I've marked the properties that I know he'd made a claim for, if you look here, they're almost like a perimeter line. My calculations are an estimate since acres are area and miles are length but each mile is roughly six-hundred-forty acres. In other words, he has marked off a perimeter that encompasses about seventy-five thousand acres."

"So, all of this eminent domain was just staged because he believed that he was going make beaucoup bucks?"

"That's what I'm assuming," Brandy agreed. "I did speak with someone from the Transportation Committee, and they told me that someone did bring up the idea of making an extension for I-95 to SR-417, but it wasn't even a consideration." She grabbed several other sheets of paper and passed those around. "I've already shared this with Reid, but the councilman who has been assisting Holbrook is actually his son-in-law."

Paris, London, and I let out a gasp. "The asshat," I practically spit.

"I'm not sure why no one else has brought this up, but it's true. Also, his son, Michael, is using threats and the official state and county symbols to make his threats seem legitimate, is enough to get him disbarred. As far as Holbrook, you can decide civil actions, but I'll let you"—she turned to Braden—"handle the criminal. I have a copy of all of this for you if it helps with your arrests."

"It will." Braden reached forward and took the stack that Brandy held out.

"Once again, I'm sorry that I wasn't able to discover the digging prior to you getting injured." I waved off her apology. It wasn't her fault, after all. "I'll leave my business card here with a copy of the papers for you in case you need anything else." She grabbed one more stack and handed them to Reid. "If you all will excuse me, I have a flight to catch."

"One more question?" I asked.

"Sure."

"What about all of the historical information I had found? Was any of that viable?"

"Actually, yes. It was my backup. The information about Osceola was priceless. The Seminole Nation will be sending elders to this area to continue your work on preserving the chief's history."

I found a little self satisfaction in those words, maybe my hours of being bored to death had made a difference and in the long run would protect us from having another person, another Johnson Holbrook try to swindle our lands.

"I really must be off." Brandy stood and shook each of our hands. "Reid, it was so great seeing you again. You look so happy here, this is where you're supposed to be." Brandy leaned forward and hugged him, but Reid didn't hug her back or bother to take his hands from his pockets. Something about his stance triggered a memory in my mind. This was exactly how he was standing on the porch that evening. He wasn't embracing her. She was hugging him. Damn it, Holland. Ugh.

While I was berating myself, Brandy had left and Reid was the only person remaining in the room but he wouldn't meet my eyes. "I've got to get back to my stables." He turned to me but still didn't meet my eyes and it crushed me. "Glad to see you up and moving, Holland." Holland? What about tiger or honey? I didn't want him to call me Holland, not now.

"Reid, can we talk?" I bit my lower lip as I asked the question.

"I think we've said enough." I let out a whoosh of air, his words stole my breath and not in a good way.

Once Reid was gone, Braden headed to the station, London took Tera to her house, I pulled myself out of the chair and shuffled back to my room. The sound of my bones popping with each swing of my arms and shake of my hips since I hadn't been moving very much reminded of a geriatric home. I crawled back into my bed and buried my head.

I got up to use the restroom. That was the only thing that made me leave the sanctuary of my bed. I even propped myself up against the headboard to eat, that was of course when I felt like eating, which wasn't often.

Chapter Nineteen

HOLLAND

When I woke up today, I had totally lost my grasp on what day it was. Reaching for my phone, I realized that it was gone. "Paris. Parissss."

"You rang?" Paris's head popped in around the half-closed door.

"Do you know where my phone is?"

"Sure do." I waited for her to finish, but she didn't say anything else.

"Care to tell me?"

"I can show you." I scowled. "It's sitting on the dining room table right next to your lunch."

"So it's noon?"

"No. It's been sitting there."

"How long?"

"You'll have to look at your phone to find out."

"Damn it, Paris, what day is it?"

"The day that you get your ass up and get moving. No more meals in bed. Take a shower, get dressed, brush the sweater off your teeth, and get out here. I'm sure that you're going to be stiff as a board from not moving. That doesn't help you heal."

"I hate you."

"I love you," Paris singsonged as she closed the door behind her.

I wasn't sure how long it took me to get ready, but I swore that I moved slower today than I had when I first came home from the hospital.

When I finally made my way to the kitchen, I was shocked to discover that it had been one week since my accident.

I slid my phone into my back pocket, ignored the plate she had left for me, and then bent over and pulled on my boots. I wasn't going to win any races, but I finally made my way to the door and was out in the fresh air. The sun was warm. I took a deep breath and coughed. Then arched my back from the pain. Nope, my ribs weren't going to let me forget that they were broken.

Gripping on to the handrail, I took one step at a time, working my way down the front porch. It was a combination of my injuries and being holed up for a week that made everything in me hurt. But I needed to see my babies.

I crept down to the stables, totally forgetting exactly how far one hundred yards really was until I had to walk in this condition. Still, something in me released when I inhaled the smell of fresh hay. To me it was like coming home.

Each step bringing me closer to the place I wanted to be above all else.

A few more steps, just a few more. Come on, you can make it.

Ever since losing Reid as someone to talk to or bitch about, I'd discovered that I talked to myself a lot more.

At least when I talk to myself, I know that I have intelligent company.

I made a mental note to use that against Reid if he should ever start talking to me again. It would be a good jab.

Resting my weight against the wall, I dragged myself along the side of the stable and then rounded the corner into the huge opening and paused. Someone, or rather some man was bent over in one of my stalls. I shook my head to clear away the pain medicine haze, okay, I hadn't been on pain meds for days, but you never knew.

I watched as the man slid his arms back, forward, then hoisted them over his shoulder. Holy cow, he was mucking my stalls. "All right, boy, your stall is all clean. I'll be back with an apple. Let me get the others finished first." My heart squeezed at the sound of Reid's voice, I had no clue what he was doing in my stables let alone cleaning them. He reached forward and rubbed my beautiful gray gelding's snout. "I know, she misses you, too." He stepped back and then moved to the next stall. "Hey there, beautiful." I smiled as Cruella leaned her head over to greet Reid. I couldn't tear my eyes away as this man, the one who I had been mean to, cleaned my stables.

"Yep, three times a day." I turned to face London, who had whispered in my ear. "He is here at the crack of dawn then goes home to take care of his own stables. He comes back midday to do the heavy cleaning and rotate a few in the paddock so they can work off some energy. Then he comes back just after dinner to feed them, walk or ride the rest, and lock up for the evening."

"But . . . I assumed that it was Braden—"

"Braden doesn't have time. Between working his own job and working overtime on the Holbrook case, I barely see him."

"What about Asher?"

"Asher is a veterinarian not a stable hand. He knows about their health, but not about mucking. You know as well as I do that ever since Wally retired, Jack has been working full-time with the cattle now." She was right. Wally had always handled all things ranch business along with London, which left Jack to help me whenever I needed him. But we just didn't have any extra hands. "I had come down to the stables to meet a guy and interview him, but Reid was already here. He said that he'd take care of it until you were back on your feet. Go talk to him. That man likes you, might even be in love with you, but if you keep pushing him away, he might just believe it when you tell him *you're not interested*."

I took a deep breath, which hurt, and nodded because London was right. I turned to tell her as much, but she was already walking off.

My feet shuffled through the hay on the ground as I made my way to him.

"Hey."

Reid set the pitchfork to the side and folded his arms. "I don't think you should be down here."

"There was stuff I needed to do. Besides, I've been locked up way too long." I took several steps toward him.

"You aren't ready to start climbing those stairs yet." He looked up to the huge flight that went up to my apartment.

"No, I reckon not. But I wanted to see my babies." I rested against the wall before taking more steps.

"Of course you did." Something in his voice held a hint of jealousy, and a small part of me felt a twinge of hope at that. "Well, I'll be out of your hair in a few minutes."

"No, please don't go." I walked closer to him. I could see his eyes, the tiny crease at the corners, and the lines above his upper lip. He was angry and fighting back the urge to say something. "I want to talk with you."

"About what? I believe that you said a lot the day I brought you home from the hospital."

"Please. I wasn't thinking straight." He raised one

eyebrow, not buying my excuse. Okay, I was using that, but it was partially true. "I was heavily medicated on pain meds. You have no clue exactly what I would have said had I been in my right mind." Reid lifted his other brow, but his face relaxed and his lips turned into a smirk. "Okay, fine, we have no clue what I'm going to say even when I'm in right mind. There, I said it. Happy now?" I rolled my eyes.

"Appeased."

"Wow, just what I was aiming for . . . to appease Reid Brooks." He let out a soft chuckle. "Just so you know, doing all of this won't get you laid."

"Good, now maybe I can get some stuff done and not worry about you hitting on me."

I laughed, pleased we could still banter. "I'm sorry."

"What?"

"You heard me, I'm sorry."

"Sorry for what?"

"You really aren't going to make this easy on me, are you?"

"Holland, to be honest, I have no clue what you're sorry for. I mean, it isn't as if you really did anything wrong. You didn't lie to me, you didn't steal from me, or cheat on me."

"No, but I hurt you."

"That isn't your fault, that's mine." Reid turned and grabbed the pitchfork.

"Don't." He stopped. "I also lied to you." There it was again, that one raised eyebrow. "I lied when I said that I didn't have feelings for you." I could hear my heart, which was weird, but I could literally hear my blood as it pumped from my heart to my veins and back again as I waited for him to say something, anything. I waited several seconds and he still didn't say anything.

Then when he turned, picked up the pitchfork, grabbed the last pile of fresh hay, and threw it into Cruella's stall, I turned around. I had my answer, which was no answer. He had nothing to say.

I had just laid my heart out on the line for what? Nothing.

"Holland?" An icy chill slid down my spine when Reid called my name. I didn't want him to see the tears that had started running down my cheeks, nor did I want to answer him. I didn't want him to hear my voice crack, so I waited for him to say whatever it was he was going to say. "I'm just about finished, can you wait for me?"

I shook my head, unable to take anymore.

"Okay, guys, sorry, you'll have to wait for apples. My girl can't wait."

What? His girl? Reid's footsteps grew closer, and then I heard the soft thump as he dropped his gloves to the ground then the warm touch from his calloused hands that were cupping my face.

He lowered his mouth to my lips, sweeping his tongue against mine as I pressed closer to his body.

When we finally broke, he stared into my eyes. "Why are you crying?"

"You didn't say anything, you just got back to work. I took that as your answer."

Reid stepped back and looked down. "I couldn't talk. You're sore, and when you told me that you had feelings for me, all I could think about was ravaging you. I needed to get this head"—he pointed to his temple—"thinking straight, so that this head"—he looked back down at the front of his jeans—"wouldn't jump you." I grinned at his obviously hard cock. "Sure, laugh now."

"I'll wait for you to finish." It took Reid less than ten minutes, and then he was sweeping me up into his arms and carrying me out the back and over to the fence. "Stay here," he ordered then jumped over the fence. He came back with a stepladder and opened it on his side of the fence before climbing back over to my side. He then lifted me over the fence and set me on the ladder before jumping over yet again and lifting me back into his arms.

"Pretty ingenious."

"I think so." He smirked.

That evening, we didn't talk. In fact, we didn't do much of anything but hold each other and watch television.

"Stop, Holland." Reid smacked my hand away for what had to be the fiftieth time. "I'm barely holding on. You need more time to heal."

I giggled at the thought of seeing how mad I could drive him.

Chapter Twenty

HOLLAND

"Hello, everyone, I'm glad that you were able to join us on such short notice." Reid stood in front of the community center's main room, and I sat in the audience, staring at my phone. We had rehearsed this a million times. "Over the last two weeks, there have been several new developments in regard to the purchase of our properties." Reid met my eyes, and I shook my head, letting him know he needed to stall. "What many of you do not know is I hired an investigator to look into the road expansion as well as the steps of due process that are required when seizing land for eminent domain." My phone buzzed, I looked down and saw my signal. I waved to Reid to give him the sign. He nodded. "It seems the Transportation Committee—" The front doors swung open and in walked Councilman Stuart, Johnson Holbrook, and his attorney, Michael Holbrook.

The three of them moved to the front of the room. "What's going on here?" Stuart asked.

"We're having a town meeting," Reid answered with all sincerity.

"We weren't notified."

"Technically, you aren't part of the town, so why would we notify you?"

Michael stepped up. "I believe this could be considered intimidation or coercion."

"Funny that you should throw around terms that would reference me as being unethical." Reid crossed his arms, ready to face off. I pressed send on my phone and less than ten seconds the front doors opened and Braden along with a detective and several other deputies swarmed into the room.

"What's going on here?" Johnson demanded.

"They're here to listen to what I was getting ready to share with my neighbors. Have a seat, gentlemen." Reid pointed to the front row.

"We don't have time for this." Holbrook moved to snatch the stack of papers off the podium that Reid was getting ready to read from but he wasn't fast enough.

"As I said, have a seat. Believe me, you aren't going anywhere." None of the men sat, which didn't really surprise me. "Where was I? Oh, yeah, it seems the Transportation Committee was never interested in building an expansion road. In fact, they weren't interested in our property at all."

"That it not true!" Holbrook bellowed.

Reid went over each carefully documented piece of information while Paris and Ellie passed out copies so that the landowners all had their own set. Every so many sentences, Johnson would protest, but it was the councilman who appeared to turn a putrid shade of green. "You see, Johnson Holbrook was after phosphate, he was looking at finding several large, key areas that he could obtain and then muscle the other residents into moving out. This would leave it clear for him to buy and then combine once the owners moved out, I believe that he was banking on this. You all have copies from the tests performed by the geophysicist he hired. Not only did Mr. Holbrook trespass and conduct testing on our properties without authorization but also he damaged the Kellys' land and left it in such a state that it could have killed someone. Unfortunately, Holland Kelly came across it and fell in, and she is very lucky to have survived the experience." When Reid was finished, he looked over to Braden.

"Johnson Holbrook, you're under arrest for culpable negligence, you have the right to remain silent . . ." Braden went through his spiel. It seemed that Braden was adding on several counts of trespassing as well. "Oh, and FYI, the DA's office already has all of this paperwork, I'm just taking you in for the basics, so I would think he will have more charges for you very soon. I think someone mentioned fraud, impersonation with the intent to gain advantage—"

"I didn't impersonate anyone."

"Actually, you did. You impersonated being a state appointed contractor to try to seize property."

I smiled because Michael and the councilman were being cuffed as well.

Call me a bitch, go ahead, do it.

I stood and clapped as Braden and the other officers escorted the three men out the door. Thankfully, Ellie joined in. I glanced over at Reid, who was shaking his head.

We stood around talking to the ranchers as they shared their thanks and said goodnight. "You ready to go home, Tiger?"

I nodded.

It was only a ten-minute ride, but even that, Reid had to hold my hand the entire way. After he pulled into his garage, he climbed out and came around to my side to help me down. For the most part, I was getting around fine, but I still hurt getting up or out of his truck. And he refused to let me drive since the strap of the safety belt rested on my right side. In all truthfulness, I wasn't sure that I could drive yet, so I didn't give him a hard time about it.

We had just plopped down on the sofa in the sunroom when Ellie came in and sat on the edge of the coffee table. "Can I talk with you both?"

Reid grabbed the remote and turned the television off. "Sure, are you okay?"

"I'm fine, really." She reached forward and patted Reid's knee. "It's actually Holland who I want to talk with."

"Okay?" I was surprised. We had always got along but we weren't the chatty sort of friends. "What can I do for you?"

"I love that you're staying here, and I truly, truly hope that you move in." Ellie leaned forward and grabbed hold of my hand and squeezed.

"I like where this is going."

"I'm not sure if you've talked about it at all?"

"No, we haven't." I looked up at Reid, wondering where in the hell Ellie was going with this.

She squeezed my hand again. "I'm not in a hurry, I just want to put this out there . . ."

"Okay?" I was a little scared of whatever she was about to say.

"When you two do get to that point, can I move into your apartment?" I burst out laughing. "Don't laugh, I'm serious. Syd lives in our apartment and yours is so cute. I don't want to move to far away since all of you are here and the closest apartments are near the university . . . yuck. Don't want to be surrounded by college kids, not to mention, where would I park my grooming van?"

"Ellie, I'm not sure you've really paid close attention to my apartment, it is tiny, minuscule." I pinched my index finger and thumb closer together.

"Let me rephrase that, I don't want to hear you two or see you two in any stage of private activity." Ellie covered her ears and then her eyes with her hands.

I let out a laugh. "Okay, when that time comes, if I decide

to move out of my apartment"—I wasn't going to say move in here because Reid had gotten very quiet—"you will be the first person I call."

"Thank you, thank you." Ellie stood.

"Is that all?"

"Yep. I'm heading out." She waved and was gone.

"Not a bad idea." Reid pulled my head over and kissed the top.

"What? Ellie moving into my apartment when I move out?"

"You moving in here. I'd love to have you all the time."

"Slow down there, buddy."

Reid brought his mouth to mine, and I smiled against his lips. Okay, maybe it won't be such a long time away after all.

Chapter Twenty-One

HOLLAND

Early May just a few months later . . .

"Get me out of here," I whispered into the phone. "I think that I just saw Scarlett."

"Scarlett who?" London asked.

"Scarlett fucking O'Hara, or maybe it was Audrey in that movie *My Fair Lady.* You know with the big hats?"

London laughed. "Yeah, I know, Eliza Doolittle. Just don't shout for the horse to move his blooming ass like she did."

"Umm, that would be arse, they were in England, after all," I corrected her.

"Just remember you're in Kentucky and trying to make a good impression on Reid's family, don't make them think we are a bunch of hicks, please."

"I promise not to eat dessert with my salad fork, but only if I can remember which fork is the salad fork so I can avoid using it. Oh, never mind, I just won't eat anything. Problem solved."

"Calm down, you'll be fine! Now, go. Be good and have fun."

I disconnected and made my way back over to Reid, who slid his arm around my shoulders and pulled me to him.

"Are you okay, Tiger?"

"Yeah, fine, just anxious to get this over with."

"Come on. My family isn't that bad."

I took a deep breath and Reid pushed open a door, a bell chimed overhead, and a woman wearing an extravagant hat greeted us, "Welcome to Steeplechase, have a drink. Let me know if I can be of help." She held out two champagne flutes.

"Thank you, we're meeting the Brooks party," Reid said as he took the glasses and handed me one.

"They're in the back."

"What is this?" I asked the woman.

"It's a mint julep." I could just hear the words the woman didn't say—*don't you know anything, darling?*

"Oh, a salad and a drink." I took a sip and tried to avoid all the green leafy shit they had tossed in. I glanced up at Reid, and he was fighting to hold back a grin.

"Like it?"

I shook my head. He took it from me.

"Me neither." As we walked to the back of the store, he set it on a table we passed. Reid pulled back a curtain to a private area, and everyone shouted.

"Reid, you're here."

I glanced around at the women sitting on large poofs. There were several small rooms off to the sides and a large dais in the center of five mirrors that made an open pentagon. When he said that his mother and sisters were picking up their Derby dresses, he wasn't lying, there were dresses everywhere. I imagine this is what backstage of a beauty pageant must look like. Just then one of the doors to a small room opened and out walked Ellie.

"You're here, thank god." She ran to me and then gripped me into a tight hug.

"What am I doing here? I don't fit in."

"It's one weekend a year, I promise. Reid loves race weekend so you're doing it for him." I nodded because I would do anything for him. "I picked out several dresses that I thought would look great on you. Sharlene"—Ellie pointed to a tall thin woman"—"promised mother that she would have it altered in time."

"We're so fortunate to have Sharlene as a friend, she is a miracle worker. She always makes a few extra dresses just in case there are any last minute emergencies or attendees." The woman, who I assumed was Reid's mother, smiled brightly as she held out her hand. "You must be Holland, I'm Sutton, Reid's mother." She kept her hands on my shoulders but turned to Reid. "Reid, she is just adorable."

Oh, great, I was now the equivalent of a puppy. I met Ellie's eyes, and she was fighting to hold back a grin.

"That is Lennon, Reid's older sister." Reid's mother said, gesturing to the woman on the far left poof before waving to the next. "That is Elizabeth, she's married to Adler, our oldest son, and the stunning woman over there is Apple, she's married to Cooper, he's just a year older than Reid." Reid's mother leaned in and whispered, "Yes, her name is Apple."

I gave a slight wave to all of them.

"Enough chatting, let's get dresses on." Ellie placed her hands on Reid. "Go. We will meet you for dinner."

I glanced at Reid, who just leaned a bit closer and whispered, "Yeah, I owe you, I know, you're going to make me pay for this."

"Damn straight," I whispered back.

"I can't wait." He ever so slowly moved his hand to my butt and pinched. I wanted to say something, but my mouth would probably give his mother a heart attack.

"So, Holland, let us see the ring," Apple practically squealed. I was going to have a hard time getting used to people saying that but I held out my left hand and showed off the one-carat simple round solitaire, it wasn't fancy, it was perfect.

"That's nice, that's real nice," Apple murmured. "But the proposal, that was elaborate, wasn't it?"

"Well, I was in his stable to see one of his horses that I'd grown attached to."

"He proposed in the stables?" She looked a bit appalled by the idea. "A horse?"

"Yes." I glanced over at Ellie and she was just smiling wide, so I continued, "He'd told me that he needed to talk to me about Hightower, but when I got there, he wasn't around. When I got near Hightower's stall, I saw an envelope pinned around his neck. I pulled it off, and saw that it was addressed to Holland Brooks." Reid's mother let out a gasp, Apple's face was scrunched in disgust, and Elizabeth looked puzzled. "I turned to go find him and ask what it was about and there he was, on one knee with my perfect ring. He asked me to marry him, and after I said yes, he told me that he'd bought Hightower for me."

"A horse? Wouldn't you rather go on a trip or something?" Apple asked.

"No." I shook my head.

Reid's mother put one arm around Apple's shoulders. "Apple, not everyone wants to travel or shop or cares about designers and fashion."

"They should."

I rolled my eyes.

"Okay, let's get on with the dresses. We've already hung several outfits for you in the first dressing room," Reid's mom said.

I opened the door and was dumbfounded. "Why so many?"

"You'll need a different outfit for each event plus a variety of hats. We have the Barnstable Brown Gala, the Unbridled, the Fillies and Lillies . . ."

I cringed but walked inside as I reminded myself that I would do anything for Reid. The room looked like Dylan's Candy Bar, there were dresses in bubble-gum pink, puffy stuff that was as fluffy as cotton candy, and hats with pieces of ribbon in a variety of colors like fruit roll-ups. That queasy feeling hit me again, but it wasn't from thinking about Reid this time, no it was pure nausea at the thought of me wearing this stuff. I wasn't a girly girl. I'd never even worn heels taller than the ones on my cowboy boots.

"You ready in there?" Reid's mother called through the door.

"Not yet." I pulled off my clothes and grabbed the first dress I saw, which was a muted purple one with blue-gray undertones. I slipped it over my head and gasped, this was a hard no.

"I heard you gasp, is that a good gasp?"

"No. I can't wear this, it's too revealing."

"Open the door and let us see." Reid's mother had that I-won't-take-no-for-an-answer tone, so I pulled the door open. The group let out oohs and aahs right before my veto on the dress was overturned.

Great.

Dress after dress, we went through the same routine. I would put it on, they would demand to see it, and then Sharlene would mark it up for alterations. When all was said and done, I had six dresses, sit hats, and six pairs of kitten heels that everyone promised even a toddler could walk in.

Each outfit was carefully hung up in a garment bag and all coordinating pieces put with it. The name of the event that I was supposed to wear it was clearly labeled. It didn't take long for his family to realize that I didn't retain information about stuff like that. I would much rather be in the stables.

On Saturday morning of race day, the guys left, and Ellie and I got ready in her room. "You think that I can get away with wearing these?" I held up a brand new pair of Corral cowboy boots. "Look how girly they are. They have all this creamy lace and they have a pointy toe."

"My mother may kill me but I think they will be adorable with your outfit. Plus your hat almost matches that perfectly."

"Really? You think so?" I prayed that she wasn't teasing me.

"I'm serious. Let me grab a thin strip of leather, and I'll see if we can maybe add it to your hat. It should pull it all together."

I pulled on the cream-colored silk dress with lace overlay and then slid my feet into my boots. If I had to be girly, I was going to be as comfortable as I could. I found some brown chunky jewelry in the bag I'd brought from home and fastened it around my neck.

Once Ellie was ready, we walked downstairs. If her mother noticed the changes I'd made, she didn't say anything and she didn't tell me to change anything either, so I considered that a victory in and of itself.

When we arrived at the racetrack, I followed Reid's family to their reserved seats, which had apparently been theirs since the early twenties. I began walking down the steps of the arena style seating and felt him, his gaze on me. I looked around and instantly our eyes locked.

My heart picked up as he moved around people to meet me. Leaning down he planted a kiss on my lips. "You've looked beautiful in the dresses I've seen so far but this one, I'll never forget."

I held up one foot. "You like?"

"Yeah, it's my favorite part. I know it's the Holland." He kissed me again. "It's my Holland." He slid his thumb across my lower lip. "I love you."

My heart picked up speed. Shit. He just said that he loved me and in public. What do I do? Were people watching? Did people hear that? I met his stare and saw a smirk on his face and then realized that I hadn't said anything in return. He was challenging me and my reluctance toward PDA. Screw that, he wasn't getting the upper hand, no way. "Oh my god, I love you. I'm so in love with you."

The end

Keep reading to discover more from this author

THANK YOU

First let me start by thanking you for taking the time to read Steadfast, this is the third book in the Iron Horse series and I loved writing about the small town where I raised my kids.

Now, let's grab some vodka and get this fucker going.

Thank you Ashley, you are the world's greatest editor, human being, and more beautiful person...ever. This is also in here because you are my editor and edit everything I write.

Thank you to the awesome Iron Orchids- you bitches rock.

Thank you again Ashley for just being you.

Thank you Julie for always fitting me in.

Thank you to all the bloggers, you help authors succeed, especially me.

MEET DANIELLE

S

Before becoming a romance writer, Danielle was a body double for Heidi Klum and a backup singer for Adele. Now, she spends her days trying to play keep away from Theo James who won't stop calling her and asking her out.

And all of this happens before she wakes up and faces reality where in fact she is a 50 something mom with grown kids, she's been married longer than Theo's been alive, and she now gets her kicks riding a Harley.

As far as her body, she thanks, Ben & Jerry's for that as well as gravity. Plus she could never be Adele's backup since she never stops saying the F-word long enough actually to sing.

LETS SOCIALIZE

Website: www.daniellenorman.com
Twitter: www.daniellenorman.com/twitter
Facebook: www.daniellenorman.com/facebook
Instagram: www.daniellenorman.com/instagram
Amazon: www.daniellenorman.com/amazon
Goodreads: www.daniellenorman.com/goodreads
Bookbub: www.daniellenorman.com/bookbub
Book + Main: www.daniellenorman.com/books&main
Official Iron Orchids Reading Group : www.daniellenorman.com/group
Newsletter: www.daniellenorman.com/news
Amazon: www.daniellenorman.com/amazon
Apple: www.daniellenorman.com/apple
Barnes & Noble: www.daniellenorman.com/nook
Kobo: www.daniellenorman.com/kobo
Google Play: www.daniellenorman.com/google

ALSO BY DANIELLE NORMAN

Although Danielle's books can be read in any order this is her favorite:

Orchids Series

Enough- Book 1 Ebook, Paperback, and Audio: www.daniellenorman.com/enough

Almost- Book 2 Ebook, Paperback, and Audio: www.daniellenorman.com/almost

Impact- Book 3 Ebook, Paperback, and Audio: www.daniellenorman.com/impact

Often- Book 4 Ebook, Paperback, and Audio: www.daniellenorman.com/often

Until- Book 5 Ebook, Paperback, and Audio: www.daniellenorman.com/unti

Under The Stars- Novella Ebook: www.daniellenorman.com/underthestars

Iron Ladies Series

Getting Even- Book 1 Ebook, Paperback, and Audio: www.daniellenorman.com/gettingeven

Iron Badges Series

Badges Prequel Ebook:

www.daniellenorman.com/prequel

Book 'em Sadie- Book 1 Ebook, Paperback, and Audio:

www.daniellenorman.com/bookemsadie

Book 'em Bridget- Book 1 Ebook, Paperback, and Audio:

www.daniellenorman.com/bookembridget

*Totally stand-alone from the above books although Ellie who appears in book 2 and 3 is referenced in Book 'em Sadie.

Iron Horse Series

Stetson- Book 1 Ebook, Paperback, and Audio: www. daniellenorman.com/stetson

Slow Burn- Book 2 Ebook, Paperback, and Audio:: www. daniellenorman.com/slowburn

Steadfast - Book 3 Ebook, Paperback, and Audio:

www.daniellenorman.com/steadfast

ENOUGH

Chapter One
Ariel

Moving to the happiest fucking place on Earth had nothing to do with fairy tales or finding my Prince Charming. Thanks to my daddy, I no longer believed in magic or happily ever afters. I landed in this city because this was the land of hotels, conventions, and destination weddings, which meant it was my best bet at becoming an event planner.

I didn't hate being a seamstress, but it wasn't my dream, it was my mama's. I never told her that I'd rather be on the other side, planning the events where people wore the fancy clothes, costumes, and uniforms.

I never got the chance.

During my freshman year of high school, she had her first stroke, spoke with a slur, and relied a little more on me. But just before my senior year, Mama had her second stroke, and someone needed to keep the business going to pay the bills, so I took over. Because Daddy was long gone, he had no use for an invalid wife, and no interest in raising a teenage daughter who hated him.

I told myself repeatedly that Mama would have wanted me to follow my dream, even if it meant hers was gone. Though, I doubted that included buying a motorcycle.

I brushed the wetness away then strapped on my helmet and headed to my motorcycle. Ever since binge watching *Sons of Anarchy*, I wanted to be badass. Okay, not like crime badass. Just the I-look-cool-on-this-bike kind of badass. So, after I unpacked my last box, I went out and purchased a Harley Sportster. I couldn't wait to start the engine and let the wind whip across my face. It was cathartic. As the engine roared to life, I replayed the words my teacher said just a few weeks ago during motorcycle safety class.

Ease up on the throttle.

Hold steady.

Don't freak.

The bike will go where your eyes go.

I found myself twisting the throttle a little more than I should have, and a small smile pulled at my lips.

I shifted gears and headed to the service road around the Mall at Millennia, Orlando's version of Rodeo Drive. Since I lived in metro Orlando, finding somewhere to practice riding wasn't easy. There were always constant road improvements or tourists who drove like idiots reversing down the interstate because they missed the fucking exit. So, the rarely traversed area behind the mall was one of the best places to practice.

It was also one of the only places I'd practiced. I stayed within a five-mile radius of my home, but I needed to get comfortable and feel confident so I could take my bike out for a long ride, let the sun shine down on my face and forget the reality that was my life.

After a few laps around the mall, I pulled my bike into a parking spot, headed inside to grab a drink, and was walking back out to my bike when two men dressed all in black cut between two cars.

They reminded me of Crabbe and Goyle from the Harry Potter movies, and I was still watching them from the corner of my eye when they broke into a run. There was nothing oaf-like or klutzy about them. Maybe they had just robbed Tiffany's or Cartier? That didn't seem right, though. There were no security guards chasing them. No alarms going off or police cruisers peeling into the lot.

Eyebrows dipping, I paused. Watching.

The two men zigzagged through another section of cars, and the one on the left pointed in my direction. In that earth-shattering moment it connected—they were after me. I ran. Fuck. I had no clue what to do. I would never be able to start my bike and get away quick enough. Their footsteps got closer then stopped. I turned around just as the two men separated, one going left the other going right, moving in an arc around me. They were corralling me like a caged animal.

"Help!" I shouted just before a hand clamped over my mouth.

"Shut the fuck up, bitch," a husky voice commanded. I didn't. I continued to try to scream as I kicked and hit him.

Biting. I raked my nails down his forearm, his face, his shoulder—wherever I could dig my nails. I wasn't going with these men willingly.

People say your life flashes before your eyes in times of crisis, when what they mean is that you replay your life in slow motion.

In those brief moments, it seemed as if I relived that day when everything seemed to unravel.

Mama sitting at her sewing table as she looked up and hollered, "Close that door. You weren't born in a barn."

And I'd had it, she kept forgiving him. "Why do you stay married to him? All day long Billie Sue Werner ran around school telling the entire freshman class that her mama saw Daddy parked by the railroad tracks with Ms. Kinney, and they were 'going at it.' It's the same thing Daddy does almost every night just with different women. You know it, I know it, the whole town knows it, Mama. And they're laughing at us."

I marched back through the house and slammed the door shut. This was just one of the many things I hated about living in a small town, everybody knew your business, and nothing ever changed.

"You go get your homework done, you hear me?"

"Yes, I hear you. But do you hear me? Mama, I'm serious. I'm leaving. I can take no more."

That was when Mama's face took on an ashen appearance and she collapsed.

I learned real fast how wrong I was, I could take more. In fact, it was shoved down my throat, heaped on my shoulders, and I was still taking it.

The brief flash from my past was shattered by the smell of days-old sweat on the man holding me. My body revolted, my mouth went watery, and my stomach lurched with the sour taste curdling on my tongue. I was going to vomit, and there was nothing I could do to stop it.

"Fucking watch it, man. We ain't supposed to hurt her, just scare her." The guy I nicknamed Crabbe had a Hispanic accent and seemed a bit uncomfortable about what they were doing.

I broke free from the Goyle-dude as he argued back.

Scare me? Scare me? What the fuck? "Help!" My shout rang out across the parking lot. "Fine. You scared me. Let me go!"

They came at me again, obviously not convinced that I was scared enough. They circled me, Crabbe in front and Goyle-dude at my back. The guy behind me wrapped his arms around my chest, restraining me and lifted me off the ground. The toes of my left shoe scraped the concrete, giving me just enough leverage to pull my leg back and aim for the fat guy's nuts.

"Help!" I shouted again and again until my throat burned

Someone had to hear me. There had to be someone! I refused to cry, not yet, not there, I needed to get a grip on at least one of these men. Anything. Anywhere. These bastards, whoever they were, were not going to get away with what they were trying to do. I had to break free long enough to pull off their damn masks, at least one of their masks. If I survived, I wanted to be able to identify these sons of bitches. I didn't get the chance, though.

Untrimmed nails bit into my ankles as the other thug grabbed my legs.

"Let's go," Goyle-dude ordered.

I bucked, twisted, and tried to get away as they carried me like a piece of furniture.

Then I heard it, a shout in the distance.

"Police! Freeze!"

In their haste to escape, the men dropped me, I scrambled to right myself and get my feet under me. My head snapped back, pain shot through my scalp as one of the men grabbed a fistful of my hair and slammed me forward. My face met the hood of a car with a sickening *crack*. The wet heat of my own blood and searing pain were the only things I registered before the man yanked back one more time. I didn't have time to put my hands up as my face barreled toward a window and I hit the car again, this time with enough force to knock me out.

I awoke on the ground, the burning hot pavement seared through my skin and deep down to my bones. Tiny pieces of gravel and sand pressed into my skin. I wasn't sure how long I'd been lying there, but I was hyperaware and could feel every single pebble and grain.

Gentle fingers wrapped around my wrist that rested at my side. I felt the brush of a watchband against my palm and scratch of calluses over my skin. Somehow, I was alert enough to process that this was a man's hand. He pressed two fingers to the underside of my wrist. It took a few more seconds to realize that he was checking for a pulse, and then the fear set in that my attackers were back.

I tried to get up, but I couldn't move, I ached too badly.

"Help," I begged, but my voice sounded like a gurgle, a sound that even I didn't recognize escaping my lips.

Lights flashed around me. I didn't understand where all the lights were coming from. My mind too clouded with fear, it took me several seconds to realize that they were prisms dancing in tiny shards of glass that surrounded me.

The hand on my wrist was gone, and a moment later, a man's face came into my field of vision.

"Can you hear me? I am Deputy Kayson Christakos; I'm here to rescue you. Paramedics are on the way. Don't try to move. You're safe."

Blink.

Our eyes locked.

Blink.

I saw stars. No . . . a star. Then I passed out, again.

STETSON

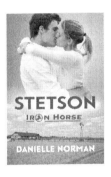

Chapter One
London

Why were funeral home's chairs so uncomfortable? Did they have a catalog of nothing but hardwood, straight-back chairs? Chairs that constantly reminded you that you were uncomfortable, the people around you were uncomfortable, and that you were going to be uncomfortable for another two hours.

Maybe they did it so that you wouldn't be distracted from the people walking by and reminding you of how fabulous your father was or how every day since you learned about his lung cancer that you worried. Nope, they wouldn't want you to miss a second of being reminded of how worried you were about not being able to fill his shoes.

Worried that you would let your sisters down.

Worried that despite everything—despite your father having raised you to believe that girls were just as great as boys—maybe the farm might have been better off in the hands of a son. That was if Samuel Kelly had had a son, but he didn't. He'd been stuck with three daughters and a wife that had run off when the girls were little.

"I'm sorry for your loss." I was pulled from my thoughts and self-doubt to accept more condolences.

"Your family is in our prayers."

"Let us know if you girls need anything."

"Your father was a good man."

Were condolences like straws and everyone drew one; whatever was written on the straw was the platitude you had to repeat?

I looked at my sisters to make sure that they were holding up. Part of me felt relieved because I knew that Daddy wasn't in pain anymore, but at the same time, I was pissed at him for leaving us. It didn't matter that I was thirty—nothing made you feel like you were a little girl all over again than losing a parent.

The pastor finished the service, and my sisters and I followed the pallbearers, who carried my father's casket out the doors of the church.

Sweat trickled down my back, and I found myself more focused on the riding lawn mower I could see in the distance than I was on what was being said as they lowered Daddy's casket into the ground. Taking a deep breath, I inhaled the scent of fresh mowed grass and impending rain. It was going to rain, I could smell the saltiness in the air, and when I opened my mouth I could taste the saltiness on the tip of my tongue.

Who was I kidding? It always rained in Florida, especially this time of the year, and the rain was always salty thanks to being close to the ocean. But right then I needed the rain, I begged for it. I wanted it to pour and send all these people scurrying for cover so that I could sit here for a few moments and say goodbye to my hero.

I was on autopilot, my focus was up toward the horizon and the rain rolling in, while people were kissing my cheek, saying goodbye, and then walking off. Person after person stopped, but I was moving out of natural reaction.

"You okay, London?" I looked at my sister Paris as she tucked a few loose strands of hair behind my ear. "You seem like you're a million miles away."

"I'm fine, just tired. Let's go home." I stood and held out one hand for each of my sisters. Being the oldest, I'd always felt a heavy amount of responsibility for them, and right then, I needed not to be the weak one.

The three of us headed to my truck. Jumping up into the seat, I paused for a second before pulling my legs in to kick off any excess dirt that still clung to my heels. Nothing about Geneva was fancy, not even the cemetery, where I had to walk through, dirt, sand, and stand in soft sod while I watched my father be lowered into the ground. After removing my hat— because in our little town you always wore a black hat to a funeral—I laid it on the console and started the engine. As I glanced into my rearview mirror, I met the eyes of my baby sister Holland, who hadn't said a word, which was so strange since of the three of us, she was always the most outspoken one.

But I wanted to get this day over with, which was probably why we had bucked tradition and decided not to have a potluck after the funeral. People from the church had been bringing food by for the last month while Daddy was in hospice. I just didn't want any more people traipsing in and out of the house telling us how sorry they were, which in the end ultimately led them to discussing the fact that none of us were married and someone was bound to offer up one of their relatives to help us out. As if we were so desperate to find a husband that we needed someone to give us their cousin's son, who was probably still living in his mom's basement and went by the name of Bubba. No thanks.

I drove the five miles to our home, the one that I grew up in, the one that still smelled of oiled leather. The smell was an ever-present reminder of when Dad would bring the saddles in and sit there with a polishing cloth, and I realized that I wasn't ready to go in, not yet.

"You coming?" Holland stood in the doorway, front door ajar, waiting for me.

"Hey, I'll be back later. I'm going up to Marcus's."

Or, more specifically, the Elbow Room, which was the bar he owned. Holland nodded, and I was back in my truck before the door even closed behind her.

Fifteen minutes later, I was pulling open the door and walking into the dimly lit space that smelled of old smoke. It had been a few years since people were allowed to smoke inside, but the scent that was imbedded into the structure assuaged me. That smell wasn't ever leaving. I remember when the previous owner had the place and my daddy would bring me up here as a kid, there were nights that the smoke had been so thick you could practically cut it with a knife. There had been no hope for the air filtration system to keep up.

I waved at Marcus, who had already changed out of his dark suit and was wearing a T-shirt with the bar's logo on the back, and slid into an empty stool. He and his brother had been two of Daddy's pallbearers, but you wouldn't have known it if you hadn't been there. He looked as if today was just another day.

"Well, I do believe I have my passport ready," he hollered. I knew that he was trying to lift my spirits.

"You may see London and you may see France, but you'll never see my underpants." I retorted, and I caught the beer he slid me down the well-worn pine top bar.

I was used to all the comments and jokes about my name, had to be. When you were raised with two sisters and you all had names of fancy destinations, people expected you to be well...fancy. They were always shocked to realize that the only thing fancy about the Kelly girls were their names. The fancy one had been our mama, which was why she ran off with the first guy who promised to show her the world when I was ten years old. She'd wanted more than farm life. But not me, I could spend my days running the fields on Madam Mim, my horse.

I downed my first beer, slammed the bottle onto the counter a bit too hard, and smiled when I realized that Marcus had been anticipating my mood and had the second one waiting. I started drinking as I scanned the room. The place was a cross between a dive bar and a honky-tonk. The walls were crowded with memorabilia from locals who had made it big or famous people who had visited. There were several photos from the movie *The Waterboy* with Adam Sandler since the bonfire party was actually filmed right here in Geneva, Florida. They also filmed a few episodes of *ER* with George Clooney here. That was when I was young and boys were still yucky, but I remembered all the moms and teachers going crazy.

M.J. Tucker, a guy I went to high school with, was sitting at one of the corner booths, and I shook my head. I seriously considered calling his wife since he was hitting on Etta Hill. She knew—hell, everyone knew that M.J. was married. Then again, we also knew that Etta's last name suited her perfectly, she was still the easiest hill to climb. Some things never changed, no matter how long it had been since high school.

"Another one, please." I turned to face Marcus to make sure that he'd heard me. He was standing behind the counter, lost in space.

I took a long swig, I hadn't realized how thirsty I'd been, two beers in ten minutes was fast even for me. Shaking my head at my realization, I followed the direction of Marcus's gaze and saw a couple of women wearing denim miniskirts and crop tops. I fought back my urge to laugh at their shiny new cowboy boots. They were wannabes. Wannabe cowgirls, wannabe older than they were, and wannabe someone's one-night stand.

Rolling my eyes, I waved a hand in front of Marcus's face to get his attention. The man always lost his shit around booty and breasts. Once again, some things never changed.

I cleared my throat and waited with a giant grin on my face.

"Holy shit, London, you just got here. You might want to slow down a bit." He cleared away the bottle but still reached behind him and grabbed me another.

"Don't judge, you know damn well that it's been a hard day."

"But you're driving." Marcus tried to argue before handing me the bottle. "Just promise me that you aren't leaving until I say so."

I chuckled dryly and nodded. Yeah, I had no intention of wrapping myself around some telephone pole.

"How you holding up?"

"Really? I'm in a bar, dressed all in black, and resembling a lost little girl. Worse yet, I feel like one. Can we talk about something else, anything?" I took a swig from the bottle and wiped my mouth with the back of my hand. Not the most ladylike action, but it was fitting for the way I was feeling.

"Have you checked out the latest *Hustler* magazine?"

"Holy shit, Marcus." I laughed so hard I almost choked on my drink. "Don't tell me you read that shit. Oh my god, I don't know that I've ever seen one."

"That's my girl, that's the laugh I've been missing." Marcus reached forward and wrapped his giant paw of a hand around mine.

"You know you wouldn't have to resort to those types of magazines if you'd stop being such a commitment-phobe. I swear that I don't know who is more sex depraved, you or the women you hook up with."

I'd been ragging on him since high school when our world was divided into two groups: helmet head or fans of helmet heads. And group two was what the helmet heads called Future Fags of America, otherwise known as FFA. Marcus and I were FFA all because we grew up on farms. But both groups had their own set of popular kids, except for Marcus, he was the one that was determined to buck the system. He wanted to sample the goods on both sides of the fence.

"Look who's talking. When was your last relationship? Oh wait, never because you are too damn committed to the ranch. You need to get out and have some fun, let loose. We need to go out sometime—you can be my wingman and help me find someone and I'll help you."

"God, I love you, Marcus, but the last thing I want to do is let you loose on my own species. You are what I like to call a man whore."

Trying to feign injury, he threw his hands over his heart and acted as if my words were causing him to have a heart attack.

"You know that does not work on me, right?"

"If you disapprove of my love life so much, then maybe you should be my dating coach, tell me what I'm doing wrong and how to find, you know, the one."

Whoosh, my beer spewed everywhere. "Fuck, warn a girl next time you're going to say something like that, won't you?"

"Is someone choking? I know mouth-to-mouth. Hey, Marcus, a bottle of beer, please."

I turned at the familiar baritone voice and tried to ignore the way it sent shivers straight to all the right parts of me. I slowly moved my eyes from his boots up his jeans, to his black T-shirt, and then to the gorgeous face. Yep, speaking of man whore, it was Braden Fucking McManus.

"You okay there, London? I'm assuming that you really don't need mouth-to-mouth."

"That's debatable, depends who's asking. If you're offering." I threw my hands over my mouth. Oh shit, I said that aloud. It was supposed to stay in my head. Beer, I had beer tongue. That slippery thing that held nothing in.

Braden coughed, making me think that maybe he was the one that needed the mouth-to-mouth and I'd be willing to practice on him.

Embracing my alcohol-infused bravado, I dropped my hand and gave him a wink instead of cowering away from my slip-up.

"You'll have to excuse her, Deputy, she's had a bit much tonight." Marcus laughed as he looked at me and tried to extract the bottle from my hands, but I held on for dear life.

"Shut up, this is only my third," I mumbled to Marcus even though he wasn't paying attention. Oh my God, this was Braden fucking McManus. I'd had a crush on him since we were in middle school. Of course, we never spoke because he was too busy being homecoming king, prom king, and the class president. He'd always been so out of my league.

I averted my gaze from Marcus and turned toward Braden. His muscled arms flexing was almost as good as watching porn. I could totally get off to this. Damn. The protruding veins made it difficult not to look at him.

Braden moved his arm to take a swig off his bottle, and it finally broke my hypnotic lock on him. I glanced up and noticed that he'd been watching me.

I gave him a head bob.

What?

I gave him a fucking head bob. The only thing missing was the Jersey accent, and I would have been all Joey Tribbiani from friends. "How you doin'?" I wasn't cool. I couldn't pull that off. What was I saying? Even Joey Tribbiani couldn't pull that off.

"So, Sergeant, what are you doing in here tonight?" Marcus continued talking as if I hadn't just made a fool of myself. I owed the guy a home cooked meal. Thank you, Marcus.

"I'm a lieutenant now. But Braden is fine. I just got assigned back to the East District, so I thought I'd pop in."

The two chatted about Braden being back in Geneva, and I sat there listening. God, even his neck was sexy.

Braden cut his attention to me. "How you doing, London? I heard about your dad. I'm sorry for your loss."

I nodded my thanks and took another swig of my beer.

"Is it true that you're going to stay and run the ranch?"

"Mm-hmm." Voice, London, use your voice, I mentally reprimanded myself. "Yeah, my sisters and I. We each have our own skills anyway. I've always handled the books and the cattle ranch, Holland is a horse whisperer if there ever was one, and Paris is a whiz with organic stuff. She keeps our fields beautiful so the horses and cattle always have new grazing areas. Between the three of us, we might equal one Samuel Kelly."

"I'm sure you'll make your dad proud."

Marcus smirked playfully as he stole glances at me, trying to tear me from my melancholy and tease me because he knew that I'd had a crush on Braden McManus since we were in sixth grade. I swallowed the lump that formed in my throat and shot Marcus a deadly glare. Braden looked at me, then nodded lightly. He had this presence about him, and it was overwhelming.

Or at least I was overwhelmed when he slid onto the barstool next to me and made himself comfortable as if he was going to stay a while. The air around me got thin, making it hard to breathe.

I studied his face a bit longer in the dim lighting of the club. He was absolutely one of those men who only got better looking with age. He was rugged with his steel jaw, which seemed to have been carved by an expert sculptor and gave him a calculated edginess. His hair was almost black and was messy in a way that could have been an accident or could have taken him fifteen minutes to get it to look like that. His mouth...oh, that mouth, it was curled into a friendly, inviting grin.

I'd bend over backward for my sisters, but Braden McManus, I'd bend over forward for.

Damn it, London, don't go there.

The trance I was in was broken when I heard Marcus faking a cough. Out of the corner of my eyes, I saw his mouth crack in to a mischievous grin. "So, Braden, how's the family?" Marcus asked as he grabbed a cloth and wiped off the bar.

"Good, Mom and Dad still live in the same house. I think that my mom is enjoying being retired, but my dad is bored as hell."

"How about your wife?" Marcus held up one finger. "Hold that thought." Marcus turned to answer the phone, which left me with nothing to do but wonder who the hell Braden had married. Was he happy? I bet she was beautiful. He probably married some cheerleader type.

"Hey, I gotta run, that was my mom." Marcus lifted the half-door that kept people from walking behind the bar.

"Is everything okay?" I leaned forward on my elbows, and my heart ached with worry for Marcus and his brother, Asher. Marcus's mom was several years older than my dad had been, and something happening to her today of all days was almost too much.

"Yeah, she's fine, but I have to run. Don't worry about your tab; they're on me. If you need anything else, just ask Jett." He gestured toward the bartender at the other end of the bar before adding, "Braden, it was nice seeing you, and I hope you stop in again."

"I'll start coming by more." Braden held out his hand, and the men shook before Marcus turned to me. "Listen to me, call your sisters or call my brother, hear me?"

"Don't worry about it, I'll make sure she's fine," Braden assured him.

I rolled my eyes and then gave Marcus my most motherly stare. "I better not find out that you skipped out for some booty call. You know that it's okay to have a dick with standards."

I turned my gaze to Braden, who was beating his chest and making a loud choking noise. "You okay there?" I patted his back and felt his body heat radiate through my fingers.

"Yep, I might be the one who needs mouth-to-mouth. I just never imagined hearing London Kelly saying something like that. The girl I remember was much quieter."

Marcus let out a loud snort. "Amazing how girls can fool you, huh?"

I shook my head, trying to clear away the thoughts of putting my mouth to Braden's mouth, and decided that one more beer shouldn't hurt, four wasn't going to kill me, it would just help get rid of that thing...shit...what was it called? Oh yeah, a filter. "Jett, can you hand me another beer?"

GETTING EVEN

Chapter One
Adeline

The screeching sound of the tires as the V8 American muscle car pulled into a parking space in one fell swoop was one of Adeline Morgan's favorite sounds in the world. The only thing better than that was shopping.

She sat in her seat a few minutes and let the song, which was playing far too loudly, finish before she cut the engine. The abrupt absence of the rumble and music in the afternoon air hit Adeline like a shiver of anxiety. There was a comfort in all things car and speed, but she was late, so she forced herself not to crank the engine again.

Adeline pushed the solid steel door open and slid from her seat before straightening her black bodycon dress, which clung on to her curvy figure. Then she slipped her four-inch black leather heels back on—one did not drive a muscle car with heels on—and grabbed the bags from the passenger seat.

The Iron Ladies office took up the majority of the fourth floor of one of the many tall buildings in downtown Orlando, and it was more of a home to her than her actual house was. The main office, like other rooms in the company, stood immaculate with white walls and floor-to-ceiling windows that revealed a large view of the city.

Adeline walked past the desks that sat in an open floor plan and into the boardroom. A large oil painting of giant handcuffs hung on the opposite wall, and in the center of the room was a large mahogany table. Around said table were some unhappy faces. Well, all except Melanie, she was pacing the room.

"Where the fuck have you been?" Melanie stopped pacing long enough to glare at Adeline. "Really? The client's been waiting nearly an hour."

Adeline shrugged and fell into her seat next to Sunday before setting her bags onto the table in front of her. "Sorry, my lunch break lasted longer than usual."

"Told you so," Sunday said a little too happy.

Adeline winked at Sunday. "No one knows me better than you do."

"Depends what truck stop we go to, I'm sure there's a few bathroom's that have poetry written in your honor and we could learn a thing or two." Olivia reached into her pocket, pulled out some money, and handed it over to Sunday, obviously having lost a bet. Sunday grinned triumphantly, tossed Adeline half the take, and turned back to her laptop.

Adeline flipped Olivia off and laughed, knowing full well that Olivia's harsh barb was only a joke.

"Well, now that we're finally all here, can we interview the client already?" Melanie asked, glaring between the two of them.

"Fine by me," Sunday said, clearly not really paying attention she was too absorbed in her computer.

"Who's the client anyway?" Adeline asked.

"Some lady." Sunday never lifted her eyes from her laptop screen.

Adeline rolled her eyes. "You think? I was assuming that we were still Iron Ladies and not men. But, then again, maybe you all voted to change that while I was out."

Olivia sighed. "How about I bring her in for the interview, and thereafter you two can argue about whatever gender you think the client is?"

"Whoa, someone's in a bad mood today." Adeline let out a low whistle.

"Adeline, you're late . . . again. You come in here with this I-don't-care attitude. But, damn it, I know you well enough to know that, if I look in those bags, there is probably something for me in there that I'm going to love." Olivia slapped her hands onto the table as Adeline leaned forward, reached into the aforementioned bags, and pulled out the most awesome black leather vest.

"I'll get her." Melanie headed toward the boardroom doors. "And for goodness' sake, Olivia. Put that thing away."

"Yeah, Olivia, put that thing away." Adeline smiled as Olivia gathered her oil rag and kit to start reassembling her baby Glock.

One of their founding and non-negotiable rules was that all four members had to be present for the first meet with all potential clients. The rule had been Melanie's idea, and according to her, it presented a professional and united front to the client.

Melanie had also stressed the importance of making a good first impression to the client, which was another important reason for all members to be present for first contact. Finally, all four members had to state their opinion and cast their vote on whether they should take the case. Majority always won. The rules may sound stupid, but it was these cornerstones that had made the Iron ladies an underground success. Oh, to most, they were just everyday businesswomen, but to the women who were passed the orchid-colored card, they were more than that.

When Melanie returned with their client, Adeline let out a muted groan. It was Loren fucking Delaney. She was everything that Adeline knew her to be—cultured, elegant, collected, classy, and the fucking mayor of Orlando's wife.

"We apologize for the delay, Mrs. Delaney." Melanie ushered Loren to a seat at the head of the table. Melanie, Sunday, and Olivia cast glances at Adeline. "I don't suppose you've met our fourth member Adeline yet?"

"Hello, Adeline, it's nice to meet you. Thank you all for agreeing to meet me." Loren gave a wave to Adeline.

"Do you have something for us?" Adeline asked.

"Oh, yes, I do." Loren reached into her purse and pulled out the secret orchid colored business card, it was the only proof that the Iron Ladies existed. They didn't advertise, they weren't listed in a phonebook, nor did they have a website. They operated simply by referrals.

Melanie took the card. "So, Mrs. Delaney—"

"Please, call me Loren."

"Okay," Melanie continued. "Loren, since you contacted us, I take it that you were given our card by one of your friends."

"Yes, by—"

Melanie held up one hand to stop Loren from continuing. "Please, we keep everyone's privacy."

Loren nodded her understanding.

"Then you also understand that this meeting is an interview and not a guarantee that we will take your case?"

Loren folded her hands in her lap, but Adeline paid close attention to the slight shake of her shoulders.

"You are aware that we are not your normal private investigator service? As such, our fees reflect our exceptional services."

Again, Loren nodded. "I really do hope that you take my case, though."

Sunday looked away from her computer and met Loren's eyes. "As you're aware, one of our services includes helping women whose husbands are . . . assholes?" Loren suppressed a laugh. "Since you're here, I'm assuming that the mayor has been very, ummm, assholey?"

"To say the least," Loren concurred.

"We need you to tell us why you are here." Melanie shot Adeline a glare for not waiting her turn.

"Please excuse my colleague," Melanie snapped. "We aren't trying to rush you."

"Well, . . . actually, I kinda am," Adeline quipped.

"Adeline." Melanie gritted her teeth.

"He's the fucking mayor, that spells trouble." A big part of the Iron Ladies success was dependent on staying below the radar, and there was nothing above the radar more than a fucking politician.

Olivia interrupted, "I think most of the talking needs to come from Loren."

"Agreed." Melanie nodded.

Loren looked down at her hands as if she was contemplating each word. "I met Greg when I was an intern at his law office. I like to think I was actually on my way to being a talented lawyer, but when Greg made me an offer to work alongside him in his organization, I took it without hesitation." Loren paused to study the faces of her audience.

"Go on, Loren," Adeline encouraged her.

"So, I worked for him as an intern. At first, I was intimidated by him since he had such temper. You know, one moment calm and the next, there were papers and objects flying across the room. He got stirred up by the littlest things. He hid it well, and only those closest to him ever saw it. Everyone else thought he was perfect. I knew he had goals to run for office, so I overlooked a lot because I knew it would be great for my career." Loren laughed, but it was a watery sound that had Olivia passing over the box of tissues they kept in the room for just that reason.

"Thank you." Loren wiped her tears and forced a tight smile. "I'm fine. Anyway . . ." She pulled in a calming breath. "We started dating a few months after I took the job, and a year later, we were married. I genuinely thought that he had loved me, but all he really loved was what I did for his image. It took me five years to figure out that the only reason he married me was because he needed a wife who fit the ideal image for his political aspirations." Loren played with the tissue in her hands, and slowly shredded it without realizing her actions. "Our marriage, it isn't real, nothing about it is real. We never talk, well, not unless we are in public, then he seems interested in me. He's a good actor . . ." Loren let out a chuckle. "Even I was fooled. Occasionally, we had sex . . . plain old vanilla, emotionless sex. But that isn't even once a month. We all know that if he isn't getting it at home, he's getting it somewhere. Every time I try to ask him about it or even ask him if he's coming home, he goes off on me. We are probably up to World War eighteen thousand in our house. Everything turns into a war."

Adeline leaned forward and gave Loren's arm a reassuring squeeze.

"The thing is, I'm tired of the pretense, of the coldness. I want a real marriage, not just something that appears perfect from the outside. I want to be happy. I want my daughter to be happy. I've endured all this time because of my little girl, and I've realized that she shouldn't be in a loveless family. I want to teach her that she deserves to be loved."

"Have you called an attorney? Why not just file for a divorce?"

Loren grabbed another tissue and played with it like a worry stone. "No, I haven't because as soon as he catches wind of this, I won't be able to fight him. If there is anything in this world Greg cherishes, it's his reputation, and guys like Greg don't allow their wives to leave them. It's as much about control as it is anything else."

This was always Adeline's least favorite part of the interview process, not because she hated meeting new clients but because this was when it felt like pulling teeth just to get a straight answer. Nothing was short and to the point.

"Do you think that Greg would try and hurt you if he found out?"

"Not physically hurt me but I need you to know that Greg is up for reelection and he has aspirations for governor someday. He views appearances as a vital part to his image. His career comes before anybody else. He can be ruthless, and when this all blows over, he isn't going to spare me. If I don't have enough to evidence against him then he will use his clout to make the courts view me as a bad mother. He doesn't want custody of Noelle, our daughter, but he'll do it just to hurt me and try to control me. Noelle is scared of him, she hides from him because he screams all the time. I desperately need your help."

Something in Adeline's gut was telling her that this case was a hard no, it was spelling trouble. "What do you think we might be able to find about Greg, what kind of evidence?"

"My grandparents owned a lot of property around central Florida and they left me a parcel of about five-thousand acres as part of my trust. It has been valued at about five million dollars and is prime real estate. Just before Greg and I got married, I had an attorney set it up for a trust for our first child. Once Noelle was born, I had her name put on the property. I asked Greg about it a few months ago because I didn't get a tax bill in this year. It always comes in my name as the custodian for Noelle. He said that he'd look into it, but when I asked about it again he got mad at me. So, I went to the property appraiser's page and looked up the information, but the info was hidden."

"Hidden?"

"Yeah, hidden. You can file to have your property address hidden on all tax records and driver's license if you are law enforcement or in a government position. It keeps people from looking you up and then showing up at your house. Our home address is hidden, but I couldn't have the land done since it was under my maiden name and Noelle's name."

"So, what are you suggesting?"

"I'm not entirely sure. I just know that something isn't right about the situation, and no one at the property appraiser's office will release any information to me."

"But, you're the owner of the property, right? Why wouldn't they talk to you about it?"

"I don't know. All I know is that when I couldn't find anything online, I called them, and the man who answered told me that he couldn't give me any information because of the Privacy Act. I tried to explain to him that he didn't need to protect my own privacy from me, but he apologized again and hung up."

"And you think that Greg has done something behind your back?" Adeline asked.

"Yes. In fact, I'm almost positive because I overheard a

conversation that he had with someone. He was on the phone one night and I heard him talking about the land. That was the night before I called you. He's the mayor, if he catches on to any of this he will discredit me, so before I do anything, I need proof that he's having an affair for the prenuptial. I need proof of his temper to keep him from taking my daughter, and I need to find out what he did with my inheritance. He is underhanded. I don't want him to be able to turn people against me and blame it on me just being a bitter woman. I want undeniable proof that he's a cheating-underhanded-asshole."

Olivia, Sunday, Adeline, and Melanie were silent for a second, waiting to see if Loren had any other bombs to drop. When the woman just continued to fidget, Melanie smiled and stood.

"Thank you, Loren, you've given us a lot to consider. We need to discuss what you've told us and do a little research on our own before we can give you our answer. We, of course, will try to get back to you as soon as possible and will keep you posted about our next meeting with you." Melanie shook Loren's hand across the table. Adeline, Sunday, and Olivia followed suit, each extending a hand one at a time to Loren.

"It was nice having this opportunity with all of you. I really hope you consider this . . . if not for me, for my daughter."

Melanie held the boardroom doors open and escorted Loren out. When the doors shut, Adeline, Sunday, and Olivia sighed in unison.

"Holy fucking shit. Loren Delaney, who would have thought?" Adeline shook her head, not believing what she had just witnessed. "On television and in the newspapers, they come across as being a happy couple. Just goes to show you that there's no such thing as a perfect marriage. What's this world coming to when women that look like fucking June

Cleaver can't keep a man? I can see the tagline now, don't take it so hard Beaver."

Olivia turned to stare at Adeline, her mouth agape. "I have no fucking clue where you come up with this shit."

Adeline shrugged her shoulders. "It's a gift, what can I say."

Melanie shook her head. "Well, let's get back to business, you know the drill." She arched one eyebrow and locked eyes with Adeline. "What do you think? It seems like you're against us helping her, Adeline." Melanie made a few notes in her notebook.

"Trouble. Politicians are all trouble. He's going to have every city office coming down on us. We are going to lose our business license and the fire marshal is suddenly going to find fifty things to fine us over before shutting us down."

"I think she needs our help and we can give it," Olivia explained.

"Don't they all?" Adeline asked.

Sunday peered over her laptop. "I liked her."

Adeline gave her a deadpan look. "I'd like to meet a client you *didn't* like. You do know we can't save them all, right?"

"Way to have a positive outlook there, Adeline." Olivia threw her hands up in the air. "Debbie downer...she delivers."

"Say what you want, Olivia, but it's shit like Greg Delaney that use their connections to rule with an iron fist. He will make an example out of us and his wife."

"Okay, Adeline, we've heard your side." Melanie turned her attention to Sunday. "What are your thoughts?"

Sunday shrugged. "I've got a feeling, I'll have the votes on my side."

Adeline scoffed. "Livi, what do you think?"

"Politician's wife. Payment shouldn't be a problem."

Melanie chewed on her lower lip. "Maybe. . .then again he could be keeping her on a tight leash."

"Love is the issue with her, not money." Sunday defended her stance.

Adeline shook her head. "We don't know that. Hell, for all we know Loren could be a great liar and actress."

"Adeline, let Loren worry about how Loren pays, okay? We've got shit to do, as long as she can cover the deposit. Besides, there's always Coco's."

"Thank god for Coco," they all said in unison. Coco was the owner of Queen's Gold a notorious pawn shop in downtown Orlando.

"Coco may not be all that willing to help Loren though, you know how she feels about cops. I don't think she holds much more respect for our Mayor Greg Delaney either."

"Well, depending on the vote, let's see what Loren comes up with first," Sunday explained.

"Sounds to me that Sunday is in favor of helping Loren. Is that right?" Melanie turned to Sunday and Sunday nodded.

"Who else is in favor of Loren?" Melanie held up her hand along with Olivia.

"Not me." Adeline was the only one not agreeing. Everyone turned to stare at Adeline amazed since she usually was the first one to want to defend all women.

"You've got a knack for being the odd one, don't you?" Melanie shook her head, once again shocked by Adeline.

"What? I don't like politicians. They're grabby. They're self-righteous, and chances are I'll have to get up close and personal with this one." Adeline shivered at the thought.

"Well, I say that we help her. She needs us and it is our job to help those that need us. Will it be risky? Yes, but that will only help us in the long run. We will prove hands down that no one in Central Florida is above us or above being busted by us. Think about it, the rumor mill that will be sparked at who actually caught Greg Delaney red-handed?"

"How about you, Olivia?"

"She's got a kid. If it was just her, then I'd weigh whether or not it was worth going against someone who had that much power and money but there's a kid involved. We do it."

Adeline flicked her nails nonchalantly as though it was no big deal that the others weren't agreeing with her. "What about you, Mel? What are your thoughts?"

"I think that while we are getting evidence to help protect Loren that we gather a little extra to protect ourselves. You know? Call it an insurance policy. He comes after us, then no matter what happens between him and Loren we have material to ruin him."

Sunday clapped her hands together. "Let's catch the lyin' lion."

"Outfox the fox," Olivia added.

"A lion wouldn't cheat but a Tiger Wood."

"Ohhh, that was badddd." They all groaned and turned to Adeline.

"What?" Adeline asked, feigning surprise. "Why are you looking at me?"

The other three let out sighs. Whether they admitted it or not, they all kind of loved Adeline just the way she was.

"Since the majority has spoken you know the rules and will have to learn to cope with your feelings. It is all hands on deck. We're going to have to do more digging than usual. I have a feeling that Mayor Delaney is especially skilled at hiding his tracks." Everyone agreed with Melanie's announcement.

"Sunday?" Melanie went down her list of notes she'd made.

"Yes, Homie?"

"You're gonna arrange a meeting with Loren at the country club, you're also gonna let her know about our retainer fee."

"At least make it our elevated fee," Adeline chimed in.

"Fifteen thousand?" Sunday asked.

Adeline nodded and so did Melanie and Olivia.

"Consider it done." Sunday gave a mock salute.

"Tires and bullets aren't cheap these days, you know? And besides we're not messing around on this one," Adeline defended her reasoning.

"Everyone got their jobs?" Melanie looked at Olivia and Adeline.

"I'll head over toward the mayor's office and start scouting the area. I'll upload photos as soon as I discover anything of use."

"I'll start trying to find out where he hangs out and if he's in to brunettes?" Adeline patted her perfectly coifed hair as she headed out to her car.

More than anything Adeline would like to throw on a helmet and straddle a motorcycle but that was unladylike and part of their formula for success was to maintain an elevated lady-like appearance in public. Her only public rebellion was her cars. Adeline blamed it on *tools of the trade*. As the lead tactical driver and instructor for evasive driving maneuvers, Adeline claimed to need powerful cars and nothing screamed power like good old American heavy duty V8 muscle cars. Plus, often times they provided the added bonus of opening conversations with their targets.

Adeline pulled into a parking lot across from City Hall and parked. Sliding on her Zoomies, one of the greatest inventions for a private eye or peeping tom, take your pick, since the hands free binoculars looked like nothing more than ordinary glasses. Adeline reclined a bit in her seat, turned on her tunes, and watched the front doors and parking lot of the mayor's office. She needed to establish a routine for the mayor.

Made in the USA
Columbia, SC
23 December 2019

85735933R00126